The wounded lawman swung frightened eyes in Calloway's direction and muttered through caked lips, "Okay, do it! Kill me like you killed Stephens."

Holstering his sixgun, Deal said tautly, "Take it easy, mister." He came in closer. "How bad is that chest wound?"

"Got trouble breathing. You ... you've got outlaw written all over your face—I expect you'll be one of those riding for the Claretons."

"I am. But no longer. I'm quitting with that mad bunch of dogs. Gotta get you to a sawbones—Saguache's east of here; sure as hell can't go there. Opposite would mean going over the mountains. Means we gotta track north around this mountain to Villa Grove."

"Why are you helping me?"

"Tired of fellin' dirty inside."

ROBERT KAMMEN
SHOWDOWN AT LONETREE

ZEBRA BOOKS
KENSINGTON PUBLISHING CORP.

ZEBRA BOOKS are published by

Kensington Publishing Corp.
475 Park Avenue South
New York, NY 10016

First Printing: January, 1994

Printed in the United States of America

One

Loneliness was a sharp knife cutting right to the nerve. After being holed up for nearly fifty days in a Lonetree line camp, the old jokes rang stale and an off-handed remark took on new meaning. The three of them knew that a late March snowstorm savaging into the Big Horn Basin had killed any hopes of their being relieved; down in the basin the trails and roads would be blocked.

Lonetree had seven thousand acres of range between Cottonwood and Fork Owl creeks, and though remote and on the lower reaches of Washakie Needles, it was ideal winter range. In the fall the three riders hazing up a small herd would stay on until they were relieved every forty or fifty days.

Deal Calloway was about the only Lonetree waddy looking forward to the enforced loneliness of a line camp. If there'd been a choice, he would have come up alone, chiefly so he wouldn't have to face the inquisitive stares taking in his burn-scarred face. Even though it was an old wound, he could feel a little pain on cold days. From just above his left ear reddened skin extended under his eye to abut his long nose and dip down past his mouth, a sort of circular patch of disfigurement, with his left cheek frozen in a grimace. The only blessing for Deal was he only needed to shave half a face. He didn't think much about it anymore.

Deal Calloway's date of birth was cloudy, but he'd been told he came out of the womb a squalling eight pounds someplace west of Scottsbluff, Nebraska. So he laid claim to the whole month of October as his birthday, his first some thirty years ago. Maybe this was what got him on the wrong side of the law down in Oklahoma and the Nations: just too much birthday and attendant celebrations.

He was solid through the upper body, rigged out as he brought his bronc laboring through a drift leather in chaps and a sheepskin to help ward off the cold. The stained brown hat was tugged low over his forehead, with a heavy scarf wrapped around it and tied below his chin. He was breaking trail for Mort Elkol riding behind.

Since noon, when the storm had left up some, they'd been out seeing how things were with the cattle they'd been able to find. Cattle had a tendency to let the wind of a storm tumble them along. Oftentimes a small bunch would blunder in to stand along a drift fence or anything else that got in their way and just hold there milling about until they died. Fortunately for these Lonetree waddies up here there was plenty of shelter.

They came to a jumble of rocks blown clear of snow by the wind, and they pulled up in the lee of the rocks to rest their horses. Burdened with additional clothing and an afternoon in the saddle, they were tired. It showed more on Elkol, who was in his late forties, and a heavy smoker, which caused him to wheeze when he talked. Mort Elkol suspected that if he went to see Doc Reese over at Meeteetse he'd find out he was a lunger. Instead he stuck to a simple philosophy of spending his wages and any spare change on tailor-mades and rye whiskey. A private bet Elkol'd made with his bronc was of his not reaching fifty. He wore a round hat squashed low so his ears stuck out, he had squinty eyes which, when they popped open more, were cut through with red veins, and he had a mottled and veined face.

Both of them could tell to within a rod or two just how far they were from the line shack, and that, dark as it was getting, three miles up along a ridgeline and through ragged timber would take them at least another couple of hours, and past sundown. The saving grace for them was that Cal Egan would have supper waiting, though it wouldn't be much since they were down to beans and the last shoulder of venison, the coffee and flour gone. Deal thought about how Cal Egan had been a caged mountain lion these last two weeks. The kid was no more'n eighteen, and he'd been gripped with cabin fever and something worse the last two days.

"I hope Cal didn't come down with pneumonia."

Elkol said, "He was coughin' worse'n me when we left this morning. Storm's about run its course. If he ain't better one of us has gotta get him out of here."

Deal looked at Elkol trying with numbed hands to shape a cigarette, and he smiled, lifting his eyes to take in the higher reaches of Washakie Needles as Deal's horse nudged at his coat pocket. Oftentimes there'd be clouds ghosting along the bony ridge of this mountain range, though it would be clear on the western slopes, and he wondered if this was the last remnant of the snowstorm, or, whether, as it often happened, another storm system was coming in out of the Pacific Northwest. He'd been in the basin going on four years, and he never took March weather for granted.

There was still an ingrained wariness about Deal Calloway. He didn't take easily to new men showing up to sign on with Lonetree; he shunned them when he could. Come summer or winter a gun wasn't too far from Deal's reach. For he never doubted for a moment that the men who'd tried to kill him would one day show up in the basin. Most men on the dodge had wanteds on them decorating U.S. marshal or county sheriff offices. Or would be keeping a sharp eye out for bounty hunters. But those after Deal Calloway were a law unto themselves, money men out of England. If the Clareton brothers respected any law or sovereign being, it was a man or corporation with more money and power.

Down in southern Colorado and Arizona he'd hired out his gun to the Golden West Land Company, which meant to Francis and Thomas Clareton. Armed with immense wealth, the brothers Clareton purchased enormous tracts of land, which sometimes included waystops or cow towns. Like a centipede trampling over everything in its path, they set their sights further north, buying land and corrupting local officials, and if anybody defied the Claretons, they turned loose their hired killers. Even the Denver & Rio Grande and Santa Fe railroads had felt the sting of the Claretons in territorial court.

As Deal Calloway had down near Saguache in southern Colorado. Somehow in the confusion after a raid on a small Mex settlement in the eastern fringes of

8

Cochetopa Pass he'd strayed away from the main bunch of rawhiders. Throughout the hot summer they'd been spreading the Clareton brothers brand of terror, but this time gunfire had cut into them in the dying haze of sundown. Deal's horse had stumbled to have the rider next to him take a blast from a shotgun wielded by a woman framed in an open doorway. Instinctively Deal Calloway had brought his sixgun to bear on the woman, but he found that he couldn't pull the trigger. Then his horse was carrying him beyond the adobe hut. He heard one of the rawhiders, Pike Gear, he determined, shouting out it was an ambush. With Deal others began pulling out of the settlement, some nursing bullet wounds and raging anger over what had happened.

With night thatching down darkly, he made his way through thick chaparral and red-loamy hills in search of the Saguache River, along which they'd guided in to hit the settlement. He couldn't shake her from his mind, the woman back there, and just why he hadn't fired back. In other raids his gun had eagerly bucked in his hand. There was always a lot of confusion, dust, yelling, no discernible order until afterwards. And even then you couldn't be certain it was your bullet that had killed anyone.

He came to a rock shelving, drew up on it, under a juniper clinging to higher rock, to stare through a scattering of yucca at a curving arm of the river still some distance away. The plan was to rendezvous back at Saguache, where the paymaster would be handing out some blood money, and where a bunch of whores were waiting. Tequila, cards, and a slut's warm body folded up to yours. So far he'd been lucky in not contacting some social disease, but even so, Deal Calloway felt

9

dirty inside. There never seemed any end to it, these raids, brought about by the insatiable greed of these Englishmen. Still holding under the juniper, though he could see movement, riders bobbing under wide-brimmed hats, on the river road, and he murmured with a curious refrain, "Wonder if any of the others are gettin' tired of taking out unarmed men, women . . . got any stirrin' of conscience."

One fear they all shared, even though they were a small army of around fifty led by gunfighter Jock La Prele, were these rumors that the U.S. Army was coming in. Probably just another hot air balloon, he mused. Or maybe not, since a few federal marshals had been killed. Most recently there had been a gun battle up along San Luis creek, in which he'd had no part. But the word out was that one if not two U.S. marshals had survived and were holed up in the mountain reaches just north of the Saguache river. A hundred silver dollars would go to the man lucky enough to bring in their heads and tinny law badges.

It was money that brought Deal Calloway's wavering mind to the hard fact he was down to pocket change. He'd be enriched once he rode into Saguache. Broke again in a few days. Stupid broke, and out again to hit some lonely outpost. Only this time, he realized, once he got paid, he had to vacate this part of Colorado. He was getting so he couldn't look into a shard of mirror in the morning. Staring back at him he'd find stony-cold eyes and killing lines etched into a face other men sidestepped away from. It was nothing for him to kill a quart of whiskey at a sitting, drunk clean through but still wary and deadly. When he spat, it coming out reeking of whiskey, his urine more of the same. Out of this

10

had come the dreams, of something tugging at his conscience, until one day he figured out his heart, his thoughts, were becoming set in evil granite, but a damned sight harder.

What was he, a quarter of a century old now, a killing animal turned loose by Jock La Prele by order of the Golden West Land Company. Unleathering his Frontier model Colt, he turned bitter eyes upon the dull-gleaming weapon. He was coming to the conclusion that a gun of some kind had been part of his life for too many years. It had become more than a weapon. It was like this Colt was a part of him, this brass and steel monster breathing out death. He jammed it back into the holster at his right hip.

"But what the hell to do if I cut out of these parts?"

The bronc responded to the jabbing spurs with short whicker of resentment when he moved it not toward the beckoning river but back around and deeper into the chaparral. Deal Calloway knew a decision had to be made tonight. If he fell in with the others he'd succumb to their talk of another wild night spent in Saguache. Doing that would render him dead drunk by midnight, hating what he was doing to himself.

In the gathering darkness the going was tough on his bronc, and he brought it along easy. Soon a half moon would light up the sky, and anyway, it was only five miles to Saguache. From the way the brush was clearing out, Deal knew he was drifting away from the river. Once distant cursing came to him, from one of the rawhiders he supposed, which only brought him forging further to the north and the low barrier of mountain.

Cowboying didn't appeal to him all that much, but he'd done that and a heap of other things since heading

11

out on his own at the age of twelve. He'd known the inside of a territorial prison, one of the credentials which had gotten him this rawhiding job. Right now there weren't any wanteds out on him. But that could change right quickly if he kept on working for this land company.

In the near darkness he could make out the yellow bunches of broom snakeweed stirred by his passing bronc and scattered mesquite humping up a little higher. The ground lifted to drop again and reveal a creek still swollen with spring runoff. The mule deer drinking up nearby some stunt pine trees didn't pick up his scent until he was almost on top of them, and his bronc bucked up a little as the deer scattered away. He didn't pick up on it at first, but knew something was wrong the way his bronc kept shying away from drinking. Then he could make out the imprints left by a man on foot, and Deal reined away from the sucking mud of the creek bank while easing out his sixgun.

His eyes stabbing about, he rode deeper under the pines, wondering if it could have been someone from that settlement they'd just hit. No, he decided instantly, not this far out. The creek curled up the floor of a wooded ravine filled with deeper shadows, and he hesitated, not wanting to blunder into an ambush. Swinging down, he kneeled to get a closer look at a footprint embedded in soggy ground. The toe of it pointed due north and into the ravine. Probably someone on the dodge, he surmised, afoot, with a posse not all that far behind.

"Dammit," Deal Calloway spat out, as he knew he was going in to check this out.

Crawling back into the saddle, he swung the bronc

12

over to bring it through thicker brush clawing at him. The bronc went at a slow walk, its ears pricking up on occasion. Then it whickered, and about the same time Deal spotted the saddled horse poking its head out from under a juniper. The horse muzzled a greeting to Deal's bronc as it jogged over, and with Deal Calloway looking about for its owner.

"No rifle in the saddle boot, and this hoss looks tuckered out—which spells trouble."

He managed to wrap a hand around the dangling reins and soft-talked the deep-bottomed bay in closer. The saddle was an expensive Texas rig. Both the bedroll and saddlebags still in place. As the horses sniffed at one another, he scanned the lower reaches of the ravine and along the creek banks. From the looks of the saddle, he pieced out, a big man had sat astride the bay. It came to him, and he tried grimacing it away, but to no avail, that the man owning this hoss had to be one of them lawmen. Probably laying further up in the ravine, probably wounded and too weak to build a fire, or too scared. Well, Calloway, you poked your nose into this, so see it through one way or another.

"Come on, hoss." A tug at the reins brought the bay tagging in alongside at a fast jog. "The bay must have broken away, so this gent'll either need tending to or a shallow grave."

The deeper blackness in the ravine was beginning to rub against the raw edges of Deal's nerves, but he held to the saddle, eyes probing for any sudden movements, the moon just starting to ease over a southeastern escarpment. The moonlight helped, if anything to add to his anxieties of the moment. Just like that he saw the barest flickering of light, up this side of the creek, now

13

the scent of burning pine. It wasn't all that late, so he knew a dying campfire could only mean one thing—another dead man lay under the prow of Aldergap Mountain. But all the same he took it easy from here on, swinging down, tying the reins of both hosses to a low juniper branch, crouching toward the campsite under more trees. A stirring ahead froze him to one spot; he could make out a crawling form trying vainly to ease more wood onto the fire to get it going. Sparks flared up now, the slender branch starting to flame, to reveal to Deal Calloway a youngish face below a thatch of sandy-colored hair. Still he held back his trigger finger, as more light spread away from the campfire starting to take hold again. The dark brown shape of a vest emerged and the shirt underneath stained with blood, the wide leather belt holding a few shells and an empty holster, and a bandanna tied around the man's thigh, a stick twisted in it to stem the flow of blood. A hand movement brushed the wounded man's vest aside to show firelight reflecting off the star-pointed badge pinned to the shirt.

Instinct brought Deal Calloway zeroing in his Frontier's for a shot. But just as quickly he checked the urge to kill. The man was no threat to him. Came a pondering notion: ease around and just leave this starpacker here to die. As he'd got a nice hoss and saddle out of it. But he held there, uncertainty rivering across his face. That lawman was money on the hoof, dead or alive. There came to Deal a long ago refrain.

". . . Be a man so dead of soul . . ."

A frustrated curse pushed the rest of it away, because he knew that breaking away from being a rawhider meant helping this U.S. marshal. He moved in cautiously, and as he did, the wounded lawman swung frightened eyes in Calloway's direction, pushed up now while trying to spin over a fallen tree in an attempt to escape. Then he slumped down and folded back down on the fire side of the tree and muttered through caked lips, "Okay, do it! Kill me like you killed Stephens."

Holstering his sixgun, Deal brushed by a sagebrush clump as his boot thumped onto a flat rock, and as he said tautly, "Take it easy, mister." He came in closer and stood looking down into a pair of gray eyes gripped with pain. "I figure you're lucky to get this far. How bad is that chest wound?"

"Got trouble breathing. You . . . you've got outlaw written all over your face. . . ."

"What I am don't matter none out here. You savvy. There's just the pair of us and a lot of wilderness."

"Yup, just you and me. I expect you'll be one of those—one of those riding for the Claretons."

At this juncture in time Deal realized a lie would serve no purpose other than to hold him to the Golden West land company. Curtly he said, "I am. But no longer. Won't cite my reasons for quitting with that mad bunch of dogs. Like today's raid, all rabied up and hit this settlement . . . only it didn't go as planned. I'm Deal Calloway."

"Webster . . . U.S. marshall," he said weakly.

"Appears that bullet's still lodged in your chest. I ain't no sawbones. How you faring?"

"Seems no main arteries are broken, or I'd be dead by now."

"Saguache's east of here; sure as hell can't go there. Opposite it would mean passing over them mountains.

Means we gotta track north around this mountain to Villa Grove."

"Why are you helping me?"

"Last week I probably woulda pumped a slug into you, Marshal. Hauled your carcass in to collect that reward money. Anyway, I stumbled onto your hoss. I'll bring in both hosses, then tend to your wounds." Deal pivoted around, risking the chance that Marshal Webster was packing a weapon and out of his fears of the moment would use it. Then he was clearing the fringes of light and honing in on the horses muzzling at short grass.

Even before first dawn was clearing away the pair of them were saddlebound. Patching up bullet wounds was an old chore to Deal Calloway. So he knew the seriousness of the chest wound sustained by Ray Webster. They should reach Villa Grove by late afternoon, a lot sooner if they could hold to a faster gait. To do so, however, would see that bullet slogging about to bust something loose, and an occasional sideways glance revealed the growing pallor to Webster's long face and the suppressed pain gripping at both his chest and thigh. The risk, as Deal saw it, was once they came around to the eastern side of the mountain, they wouldn't be skirting all that far north of Saguache, and just could run into some of Jock La Prele's men. They'd expect him to be packing a dead marshal slung over the other horse and pointing more southerly toward Saguache.

He'd explained this to Marshal Webster, who'd said, "You could pull out and leave me if this happens."

But for Deal Calloway it was with the realization a turning point had come in his life. Once he got this U.S. marshal in to Villa Grove, and despite his loathing of cold

16

weather, he would strike northerly. And as it warmed toward noon, they could see the more blunted eastern edge of the mountain drifting into view, a wide basin opening up to them, and a noonday haze shimmering over the Sangre De Cristo which loomed across the far reaches of the basin. Closer in, around them, there was a quiet serenity, a few birds wheeling about, their horses jogging along, but with Deal casting wary glances southeasterly.

Under a shading juniper they held up, the heat rising around them and sapping at U.S. Marshal Ray Webster's strength. He folded himself over the saddle horn, taking the canteen from Deal with a grateful hand. Though he was thirsty, he drank sparingly as of a man hurting deep inside or one with a lot of grit. To judge by his appearance, Ray Webster was in his late twenties, sparse and big boned. He had an Oklahoma drawl and a way of spacing out what he said; by this he showed himself to be a man who measured things carefully. Unless, Deal mused, it was just the pain getting to him.

Deal offered, "We could lay up until it cools some."

"I don't want to have to get on this hoss again, at least in this condition." There was an apologetic smile as he coughed up a little blood. "Twenty miles further, you said."

"About that," replied Deal. "Sorry I didn't pack along any whiskey." And Deal Calloway wished he had. His nerves were tingling; the heat was drying him out and cleansing the liquor out of his system. He'd been on a drunk going on two months now, starting at sunup and nipping at a bottle during the day, a habit shared by the other rawhiders. It had helped to numb his memory of what they were doing, but all the same he hadn't been able to shake away the wrong of it all.

17

From the scattering of juniper and chaparral to the southwest he brought his eyes back to Webster, who was still slumped forward in the saddle. Deal swung down and untied his lasso from the saddle. He coiled it around the lawman's waist, and then to the saddle horn, saying, "That should keep you from falling off, Marshal. This'll be our last rest stop. 'Cause if we don't push it from here you just might cash in your chips."

This produced a trusting nod from Marshal Webster. "So be it, Calloway."

Back in the saddle, Deal shot a brief glance at the Winchester thrust in the marshal's saddle scabbard. That made two rifles he'd need if they chanced to encounter any rawhiders. Far to the south he could make out a rising mesa behind which lay Saguache. The way they were heading, northeasterly, would have them crossing one or two watery fingers extending out from Saguache Creek. Beyond that it was all plains to their destination. But along the creek there were sunken places that over the years had become hidden tar pits, and where a lot of animals had become entrapped. He shoved the worry of this aside as he said to Webster, "You just hold on to the saddle horn." He reached to take Webster's reins. "We got this far, we'll make it the rest of the way."

Some three miles later they passed through soggy ground and drying mud passing along a creek bed. Here and ahead there was more scrub brush. The sky was a steely blue color, and their horses still cantered along easily. What troubled Deal now was an arm of a creek ahead. He could avoid it by angling due north, but that would tack on a lot of miles, so doggedly he kept on a direct line toward the fringe of brush and the creek. He swung an anxious glance at his saddle companion, and as he did so Deal Calloway failed to pick up on a bunch of riders ghosting out from under scrub trees running along the creek and no more than two hundred yards away.

"Yo, Calloway!" one of them yelled.

By sheer force of will, anger piercing into his eyes, Deal stilled the impulse to swing about and break away. He should have taken the safer route to the north, but it was too late now as he was in amongst the encircling outlaws. One of them, a jayhawker named Ridley, swung in closer as he spat out, "Damn, if Calloway here ain't bagged himself a U.S. marshal." He grabbed Ray Webster by the hair and yanked him erect in the saddle.

"Maybe so," said a bony-faced man clad in shades of gray clothing. He was Jock La Prele, renowned as a gunfighter and killer of at least fifteen men. He wore two sixguns, and a black flat-crowned hat shaded his pondering eyes. "Doesn't make sense, Calloway, your wet-nursing this lawman. Or where you've been since last night? As you sure as hell weren't headed for Saguache."

"What about this lawman?"

Jock La Prele said calmly, "We'll leave that up to Mr. Clareton. Disarm both of them."

When they were clearing the brush, Deal Calloway took note of the tent pitched on the other side of the creek and the large black horse hitched to the fancy buggy. But of more interest to him was the man lounging in a chair resting under a shading tree. While his brother Francis stayed behind to tend to business matters, oftentimes Thomas Clareton went along with the rawhiders. The only man allowed access to the English-

19

man was gunfighter Jock La Prele, who led the way across the narrow expanse of creek. As La Prele came in on the tent, a woman emerged from it, combing away at brownish hair spilling to her waist. Her frosty eyes went from the gunfighter to the others spilling into their campsite, and now to the three rawhiders guarding Deal Calloway and the lawman.

Deal knew the woman had been Thomas Clareton's companion for about two months now, would probably in the not too distant future be replaced by another, and then by still another. He couldn't make out what La Prele was saying, but from the look of displeasure on Clareton's face there came this queasy feeling, and he swung his attention to Marshal Webster.

"I don't want you lying for me, Marshal."

"I'll say it straight, Calloway. That's ... one of the Claretons."

"A proper English bastard," quipped Deal. He turned stony eyes to Jock La Prele and the Englishman, who were walking his way. Clareton was tapping a riding crop against his heavy tweed riding trousers, and dust misted his black boots. He was tall, around six-one, with aquiline features and haughty eyes sparking out how he felt. The white shirt he wore was open at the collar, and he had a stolid frame.

"Calloway, is it? Yes, I expect you were bringing this U.S. marshal in just to collect the reward. If so, very commendable, Mr. Calloway. But, unfortunately, Mr. La Prele thinks otherwise."

"He's hurt bad," Deal said. "There's a doctor in Saguache."

"By bringing him here, Calloway, you have put me in a rather precarious situation," Thomas Clareton mur-

20

mured offhandedly. "You men, divest our guests of their horses. Tie them to those trees."

"Why bother with doing that," muttered La Prele.

Clareton, stepping closer to the gunfighter, said softly, and through a pensive smile, "Naturally they cannot bear witness against us, Mr. La Prele. But to just kill them out of hand." He began moving toward his campsite. "There is a form of punishment I was witness to in India . . . something that you might find amusing."

The day wore on for Deal Calloway, who was hogtied to a tree trunk, while lawman Ray Webster, sagging heavily against the binding rope, had lapsed into unconsciousness. Deal knew that Webster wasn't going to make it, even if they got as far as Saguache. The Englishman had talked La Prele out of killing them, the disagreement was only over the timing. The Claretons, they killed people with their land deeds and money. Now, with the killing of another U.S. marshal, they had placed themselves above the law. Now Deal flexed his hands against the rope cutting into his wrists. There was some give, and though his skin was rubbed raw, he kept at it.

He responded to a low moan from Marshal Webster by saying, "Try to hang in there. They're getting liquored up and just might forget about us."

"Water . . . please, please someone . . . help me. . . ." He cast a blind glance at Deal Calloway, trying to focus, to make sense out of all of this, fighting the numbing pain. Something in Ray Webster was telling him he was dying. His lips quivered, but no words came out, and he sagged down again.

"Damn," Deal spat out, as he twisted to see back around toward the creek where the rawhiders had

21

pitched their camp, some fifty yards deeper into the scrub trees. Even if his shout echoed into their camp, none of those miserable rawhiders was about to break away from his bottle of whiskey or card game.

One thing that had puzzled Deal after they'd been tied up here was that Jock La Prele had headed away from the Englishman's tent and to the main camp, and shortly thereafter some of them had put together a large fire, while others on foot sulked along the creek as if searching for something. La Prele, on his way back toward the Englishman's tent, had detoured over to look in on his prisoners and gone on just as silently, and Deal's eyes had been drawn back to the creek bank. He could make out two of them sunk down digging away, others clustered around as daylight passed into dusk, and then one of them heading back to their camp holding a coffee pot.

"That creek's nothing but alkali water?"

A shift in the wind ruffled at Deal's hair, brought with it a strange acrid scent. What was it he couldn't remember? The wind picked up stronger, rustling branches, the full force of the growing scent splashing across Deal's face. And he exclaimed, "Those tar pits. It's tar I smell?"

The implications of what this meant caused him to sag down, choked with fear, wishing now that Jock La Prele had used his gun on them. He looked at the lawman hunkered over and hoped right now that Webster was dead, so's to spare him the dreadful agony of what was to come. If Deal judged the Englishman correctly, hot tar would be poured over them. Afterwards a flaming torch would turn both of them into Roman candles. Deal Calloway shuddered and attacked the imprisoning rope with a vengeance, feeling it give some more, cursing it, just letting go of his pain in an attempt to free himself.

Finally, exhausted, sweat peeling down his face, he gasped in cooling night air, sucked it in deeply. He shook away the drops of sweat stinging his eyes, taking in what he could make out of the Englishman's tent. The woman and La Prele were seated there too. The muted bark of Thomas Clareton's strident laughter slipped through the trees, and around the tent and from it was a halo of light. It was whiskey laughter Calloway had heard, not only from southerly but from the main camp of rawhiders. But drunk or sober, Deal knew these men would have their sport with him and the U.S. marshal.

Reinforced by this knowledge, he began working at the rope again, felt it give even more, and hope flared in Deal's eyes, only to fade away at the tangy sounding of a hunting horn; that was the Englishman's way of summoning his hired lackeys. And they came in an eager mass, away from the main camp and from behind the tree holding Deal Calloway prisoner. The Englishman stepped along lightly with the woman holding to his arm and the gunfighter matching Clareton's expectant stride through the scattering of trees. Ignoring the stirrings of the lawman, Deal found that he could wiggle one hand free, and his left now, but he was still entangled somewhat with the riata, which was tied behind and around the tree, and a couple more coils entwined his chest. He held still now as men he'd rode and killed with came in to form out a little ways an amphitheater of grinning, wolfine faces. It was Ridley, the one who'd plucked away his Frontier's, who came in close holding

23

onto a coffee pot filled with hot tar, and Ridley swung it close to Deal's face.

"What they call, s'thern coffee."

Grittily Deal said, "You're nothing but a pimp and whore monger." And to himself he said, *just come in closer, damn you, so's I can grab that sixgun out of your holster.*

Snarling his anger through bared teeth, the rawhider brought a gloved hand to the bottom of the coffee pot, and then he swung it at Deal's face. Deal Calloway tried to swing his head away from the black mass of hot tar reaching out at him. The stench of burning flesh filled Deal's nostrils, along with a pain so unbearable that he broke out screaming as the hot tar ate away at the side of his skull.

Through the screams of one man came the shout of another, of the Englishman yelling out as he pointed at the rawhider gripping the coffee pot, "Kill him!"

At first Ridley didn't hone in on it, turned as he was to gape at Thomas Clareton, and when gunfighter La Prele's Colt sprang out of its holster, Ridley was expecting to see a bullet punch into Deal Calloway. Too late the truth of it dawned in Ridley's mind. He sent a frantic, drunken hand stabbing toward his holstered gun even as the gunfighter's Colt spat out flame. The rawhider took the slug just where his ribcage tapered around his belly, the force of it spinned him sideways and down. He lay there, his buttocks protruding up, and with both hands groping to stem the flow of blood. La Prele's gun sounded again, and a second slug punched up through the crack in the rawhider's Levi's.

A silent scream tore out of Deal Calloway as he writhed in agony. *Do it, La Prele, turn your gun on me.* The shock of it was blacking everything out, and he could barely stand.

The Englishman said loudly, "I expect my men to behave properly. Otherwise Mr. La Prele will be called on to use his guns again. You there, bring me that bottle of whiskey." He stepped in closer to U.S. Marshal Ray Webster, who was trying to lift his head. When he managed to do so, his eyes fluttered open, and then the Englishman was there, lifting the bottle to the lawman's mouth. "Drink as much as you want, Marshal. That's it. Drink some more."

Marshal Webster blinked away the blurriness, and as Clareton's face began to focus in his eyes, with it came comprehension and Webster's weak voice, "You're . . . Clareton . . . you damned . . ."

Thomas Clareton lashed out with his riding crop, and again he brought the heavy leather object lashing across Marshal Webster's face. "You have insulted me, sir." He threw the whiskey bottle away and brought the crop up to punch it into under the lawman's chin. "You have brought malicious and untrue charges against my brother and I. I cannot tolerate such behavior." He stepped away and caught Jock La Prele's eye.

The gunfighter turned toward a man holding a canteen filled with hot tar. Behind him a rawhider held a lighted torch, and at his feet were other canteens and a coffee cup from which came the vaporous odor of tar. Gingerly La Prele wrapped a glove hand around the canteen as he said, "You boys, latch onto them canteens."

He stepped past the Englishman and for a brief moment gazed into the lawman's eyes. It wasn't the pallor so much as a certain glimmer in Webster's eyes that sig-

25

naled to La Prele the man was dying. But all that mattered to the gunfighter was that this damnable lawman could still feel pain. Though the heat from the tar was beginning to burn through his glove, the gunfighter let the contempt he felt for this lawman sweep out of his eyes. The Englishman, he realized, had been right. A bullet would have been too merciful.

"You bastards have dodged my heels for too long," Jock La Prele said bitterly. "You think your horseshit laws give you the right to trample over those such as me." He brought the spout of the canteen up to Ray Webster's mouth. "Have a drink of hot tar, lawman."

As the hot, black syrupy liquid spilled into his mouth and on his face, Marshal Webster tried jerking away, his eyes wide with fear. Then the indrawn gasp of pain gave way to a piercing scream as hot tar began spilling onto his head, burning, searing, finding a crease in his forehead and filling an eye socket. As soon as La Prele's canteen was empty, he stepped away, and another rawhider poured more hot tar onto the lawman's shoulders. The tar ate away at his clothing as it sought entry to the flesh underneath.

It was here that Deal Calloway realized every eye was riveted on Webster, the man writhing and screaming out his agony in his final death throes. He had managed to free both of his hands, but held them behind him, watching in dreaded fascination now as the man with the torch brought the flame in to ignite the tar coating Ray Webster's head. Quicker than the strike of a sidewinder the head and upper body dissolved into one fiery ball, the flame spreading down. It was here that Deal spun back around the tree and broke through some low bushes. He was halfway to the creek before anyone noticed he was gone. Above this babble of confusion of voices came that of Thomas Clareton, high-pitched and filled with terrible fury, "Go after him, dammit! Kill him! Kill that damned turncoat!"

It took Deal Calloway a moment to realize it wasn't the heat coming from his burned face now but the brush of a wintry gust of wind blustering up snow around him. And that he was a long way from Colorado. He shouldn't have let himself go like that, reliving his outlaw past, but sometimes it just happened. He'd heard of Civil War veterans living with the nightmares of the killing grounds for years, and this wasn't any different. The past could age a man faster than anything, and as for tomorrow and beyond, just getting to the line shack was all the future Deal Calloway could think about at the moment.

A tug at the reins brought the bronc angling along a vague trail cutting up a shaley slope. It was tough going, and getting a lot colder in these shadowy recesses of mountainside. The bronc lunged onto a flat expanse of plateau tapering away to show the farflung reaches of the basin. Here the snow was deeper, with boulders poking up like mossy landmarks around which they brought their horses. As he rode, Deal looked due northwest, where chimney smoke peeled over some birch trees, a comforting sight. The line shack was still about two miles away, with a sunken draw ahead which Deal knew would give them trouble in clearing because the snow had a tendency to really pile up in there. Habit made his eyes search for cattle in a sweeping glance down to the foothills where trees thinned out. Instead he found himself spearing in on a faint glow of light, and he reined up quickly.

"What's up?" questioned Mort Elkol. He watched Calloway pull a field glass out of his saddlebag.

At first he couldn't find the source of that light, then it danced into the magnified eye of his field glass. It was a large campfire, Deal found out, and he counted at least nine men squatting in close. Too far north, he mused, and too many of them to be from Lonetree.

By way of confirmation Elkol said, "They sure as hell ain't from Lonetree. A posse?"

"I make it that way. When this storm hit they holed up someplace. Same as did those they're after."

"There ain't no way over these mountains; so come sunup they'll be heading south." Elkol grimaced through the vague light. "Probably a bank holdup. Never had me no account with no bank. How about you, Deal?"

"I ain't seen the insides of a house of prayer or a bank since I was goin' on ten, I reckon." He matched Elkol's red-cheeked grin with a smile. "I did take note of the fact it was a banker passing around the collection plate in that Baptist house of prayer. There's that draw ahead, Mort. Trouble no matter where we tackle it."

"Lucky it ain't all that wide, just a trifle deep." He brought his horse in the wake of Calloway's, savoring the heat of the line shack and hungry enough so that even a boiled leather halter didn't seem all that bad.

What roiled through Deal's mind was not that distant campfire so much, as it could only be some lawmen. His worry was that Cal Egan might be entertaining visitors in the form of bank robbers. He saw no need to express his worries to Elkol.

The snow up here at times came up to the belly of

their horses, which plunged ahead to throw up snow snatched away by the moaning wind. Along the draw rose a few pines, and Deal reined downslope for a couple of rods in search of a place to cross. Right about here, he decided, swinging his horse away from the draw and then reining it around.

"Okay, hoss, you've done this before." He spurred the bronc back through the tracks it had broken in the snow and into a gallop. The bronc cleared the first reaches of the narrow depression, then it struck into deep snow and began surging forward until it came out under some pine trees where there was barren ground. In short order Elkol managed to bring his bronc across, and Deal said by way of warning, "We might not be the only ones who've sighted smoke coming from the line shack."

"It would be a tough haul up here with all this snow."

"Yeah, but when you're riding the highlines a man'll try latchin' onto anything." He swung his bronc around and peered, under the high branches of the pines, at the roof of the line shack which showed over a nearby rise. "Along with Cal's two hosses, our spare mounts are a clear sign that Cal ain't loning up here."

"They could have stolen our hosses and lit out, Deal."

"Expect they could have. Only one way to find out." He rode out from under the trees and up the short rise. What he sighted in on was an extra horse in the corral. "Just one man. Mort, hold here and cover me with your rifle."

"Don't you get careless, Calloway. You know, Deal, it could be that banker you talked about come up here just to pass around that collection plate."

Deal made no comment as he kept on this side of the rise, letting the bronc pick its way through finger drifts, and now he came over the rise and into the back of the line shack.

The one window spilled out light through the oilskin pane covering it. He pulled up in back of the corral, swung down, and left his bronc there. His Frontier's in hand, he went up to the back window to peer through a crack in the oilskin at a man seated at the log table and wolfing away at a small hunk of venison. A rifle lay across the table. But where was Cal Egan? His range of vision was limited to the table and north wall, the bunks situated opposite. Hooking a finger in the oilskin, he made the opening a little later, and then he saw Egan strung up like a side of beef.

The cowhand's head was sagged down and his sightless eyes fixed on what was left of his chest. The skin had been peeled away down to his pubic hairs, with blood staining in and forming drying puddles on the floor. Taking in the horror of this, and now realizing that Egan's left ear had been hacked away, Deal shuddered in revulsion as he backed away from the window.

All he could think about now was of how Egan must have suffered. He'd known pain, but nothing compared to this. Calm reasoning took flight from Deal Calloway like a magpie rising in alarm from the bloated carcass of a dead horse, and he came around the corner of the line shack, thumbing back the hammer on his Frontier's, possessed with the need to settle the score.

Blundering through a drift and around to the front of the cabin, he came in on the latched door. He brought a spurred boot smashing into the door, and when it sprang open, there was the outlaw making a grab for his rifle.

Deal Calloway didn't hesitate but emptied the loads

from his sixgun into the man who'd killed Egan; most punched holes in the man's upper body; a couple found the head. The man flopped down to splinter the chair away. Somehow Deal realized the hammer of his Frontier's was thudding onto an empty chamber. But if he had been wearing a second gun, he would have used it, even though he was dimly aware that the outlaw was dead.

Shoving his sixgun back into the holster, he stepped over the threshold and bent over to take hold of the dead man's hand. He dragged the outlaw outside and around to the side wall, and when he spun away from the body, coming in was Mort Elkol, who spat out in awed terms, "I ain't never seen shootin' like that." Elkol swung down, questions dancing in his eyes. But from the set to Calloway's face he knew the answer to all of this lay in the cabin.

Mort Elkol let his reins drop as he crunched through the snow and pushed into the line shack. He took one long, disbelieving look, and when he swung around, he couldn't frame words to express how he felt.

It was here Deal took charge. "First we'll tend to our hosses. Then we'll cut Egan down and wrap him up in his bedroll. We'll see he gets a proper burial at the cemetery over at Pitchfork."

TWO

By sunup the wind had followed the last of the clouds out of the Big Horn Basin. But during the night snow had blown in to block against the cabin door, and it took the pair of them to force the door open enough so that Deal Calloway could get outside.

Snow was sculpted into knife-edged drifts and lay sparkling and bowing down the branches of pine trees. The sun was still ghosting low to the east, but even so, from the feel of it Deal knew it would warm into the thirties. He reached the corral and looked in at the horses nibbling at hay stacked up under the lean-to attached to both the line shack and one side of the corral. They seemed contented, knowing the weather was going to change, and Deal moved back to the corner of the line shack and picked out one of the shovels leaning against the log wall. Briefly he studied the toe of a boot sticking out of a drift. There weren't any feelings of remorse. And he'd let those lawmen dig out the corpse.

He came around to the front of the low cabin, and before shoveling away the snow blocking the door, Deal took in the moving specks, black against the snow, working their way up an arm of Cottonwood Creek. By rights he should dig out the body, pile it on the outlaw's horse, and let Elkol take it down and hand it over to that posse. But as he'd explained to Mort last night, he wasn't seeking any notoriety or reward money.

"The way you're standing there them lawmen must be coming up—"

He looked over at Elkol's head poking out of the door and muttered, "Be here around noon." Then he bent to the task of shoveling snow.

It was around 11:30 when Deal Calloway, astride one of his broncs, took in from the shelter of some pines Sheriff Elmo Cowley coming in on the line shack trailed by a scattering of horsemen. Out front to meet them was Mort Elkol. It had also been decided between them that Elkol would see that Cal Egan's remains were brought down to Pitchfork and that Deal would hold up here until the relief crew arrived from the home ranch.

From his vantage point in the trees the voices of the riders carried up to Deal, especially Cowley's low frogy drawl, as if everyone was sharing the same room. The posse pulled in around Elkol and some of them dismounted as Mort Elkol began his veiled telling of last night's violence. Listening, Deal let his eyes flick over a lot of men he knew, and some he didn't. Now they got to squinting in on one rider who'd been hanging back and shielded by those crowding in around Elkol. He snapped silently, "A woman?" He watched the way she dismounted, his thoughts distracted by her presence.

"So it was Deal going in while you covered him."

"Yup," confessed Mort Elkol. "The same thing coulda happened to us. What was this Ridley wanted for?"

33

"Killed a man in Elk Basin . . . and got into another killin' ruckus at Meeteetse. You said the body's over by the side wall?"

"Out enjoyin' this nice spring day," grinned Elkol. "The hell of it is, Elmo, we're about out of coffee and grub. Hope you boys brought along something."

"We'll make do."

Higher on the slope, Deal Calloway brought the bronc around to head away screened by the trees. Ridley, he mused, wasn't all that common a name. The Ridley he'd known down in Colorado was about the same size, but younger and didn't have a beard. But, he pondered, he hadn't gotten a good look at the face of the man he'd killed last night, nor did it seem particularly important at the time. Maybe he'd been blinded by that red killing haze, his mind still filled with the horror of what had happened to Cal Egan. His intentions of the moment were to mosey around this plateau to check out the cattle, and when he returned at sundown he expected everyone to be gone. In the days to come he'd wish time and again he'd held on at the line shack. If he had, Deal Calloway would have learned that it was indeed the same Ridley that he'd ridden and killed with down in Colorado. And that the woman was the sister of slain U.S. Marshal Ray Webster. Right now, though, all Deal wanted was to get around this outcropping and down into a dense stand of limber pines.

The woman's name was Cleo Blaine. Only within the last year had her search for the men who'd murdered her brother brought Cleo Blaine up into Wyoming. She gazed stoically at the frozen body of outlaw Bat Ridley.

How desperately she'd wanted to rip the truth out of Ridley, not only about how her brother Ray had died, but to learn how other lawmen she knew had been so callously murdered.

The last three years had seen her reach the thirty mark. Cleo's face had lined more, and there were some days when she wished she was back in Oklahoma City, just tending to the chore of being a banker's wife. That her husband still bankrolled her efforts to find these killers told of his love. Over a year ago the clues had begun drying up, as the land company owned by the Clareton brothers had gone out of business, or so it had seemed at the time. Rumors had it they had gone back to England, with other stories saying it had been down to Capetown, even Australia. She did know that the Colorado territorial governor had sent lawmen bearing extradition papers over to England.

The rawhiders working for the Claretons' Golden West Land Company had scattered out about the same time, but Cleo and her brother, Dave, had tracked some of them down. Ray's death had stilled Dave Webster's high hopes of hooking on as a U.S. marshal. Ever since, like Cleo, all he'd wanted was to exact revenge. And he had, taking out three of those who'd ridden with Bat Ridley down in Colorado. The horse under Dave Webster had a wide chest and it stood a couple of hands taller than the grulla ridden by his sister, as he was a big man. They'd hired on a couple of men handy with a gun down in Colorado. Joe Cholach, one of those dismounting by the corral, had been a deputy sheriff out of Pueblo County, Colorado. Come the fall elections of last year a new sheriff had taken over, cutting Cholach adrift. Shortly after this he came riding into Stone City in response to a newspaper ad put out by Cleo Blaine. The other man was a Kansan named Hank Wardell, lean as Cholach was, but somewhat older, with a salt-and-pepper beard. These two were the last of about a dozen that Cleo Blaine had hired to help in her search for her brother's killers. After a while some had quit, or as had happened at Antero Junction, in an exchange of gunfire, a few found they just didn't have the stomach for this kind of thing.

As Dave Webster swung a leg over the back of his horse and swung down he took in Mort Elkol and a couple of others carrying a blanket-wrapped body out of the line shack. The talk fell away, and Sheriff Elmo Cowley removed his hat to wipe sweat away from the sweatband even though it wasn't all that warm up here yet, maybe into the low thirties. After the job of tying Cal Egan's body over the back of a horse was finished, there was a general move to go into the line shack. But holding outside were the sheriff, Cleo Blaine and her brother, Dave.

To start the conversation again, Sheriff Elmo Cowley said, "Happens this way sometimes, a man gettin' gunned down for no good reason."

"Some men don't need any reasons."

He nodded at what Cleo had said, frowning now when he cast a glance downslope. There wasn't much wind yet, and it would be a blessing if they didn't have to fight any kind of wind when they retraced their way down into the basin. This Cleo Blaine was kind of pretty, he mused, but inside she must be hard as anviled steel. Had to be to keep going like this. This was the first time a woman had been part of one of his posses, but back at Meeteetse she'd been more than willing to share the risks.

"You know, ma'am, it'll be Elkol and Deal Calloway coming into any reward money."

She speared Cowley with a smile showing even rows of teeth, but there was no joy in it, for Cleo's eyes were dimmed with sadness. The extra clothing made her look bulkier, and her russet-colored hair was pinned up under the low-crowned hat. Except for a picture of Anne Oakley adorning a poster down in Meeteetse, this was the first time Cowley had ever seen a woman wearing a gun belt. He didn't doubt but that she knew how to handle that .32 Smith & Wesson.

"I'm not interested in any reward money."

"You didn't tell me all that much about this land company Bat Ridley worked for."

"Any sheriff in southern Colorado," said Cleo Blaine, "could tell you more than you wanted to know. Ridley, the others we're after, they all are wanted by the law."

Dave Webster said wryly, "All but one of them. We don't even know if this man is still alive." He looked at his sister, and at her reluctant nod, Dave Webster went on to tell Cowley just how their brother had died. "Men who would throw hot tar on someone . . . then set them afire . . . can't be anything crueler or more evil. This rawhider we caught and turned over to the law, he told about this, and about this other man, one who rode with them, trying to help my brother. These rawhiders were fixin' to do the same to this gent, only he managed to get away. But he was burned badly too, sheriff, up around his head."

"I see," murmured Sheriff Elmo Cowley. He could see the pain etched on their faces, and right now he didn't want to build up their hopes, although the man who'd helped their brother might be Deal Calloway. Hadn't they said this man wasn't wanted by the law? He turned slightly to keen his eyes to the wide sweep of this high plateau in search of any glimpse of cowhand Deal Calloway. This would explain why Deal had cut out, why he rarely showed up in town. But until he found Calloway and sounded the waddy out, he'd best keep this to himself. To the woman he said, "Guess I didn't pay much mind before, down in Meeteetse, when you spoke about some choice land being bought up."

"A lot of land, Sheriff," she said as Mort Elkol hollered out the line shack door to come in and get to eating. She fell into step with Cowley. "As I told you before, land agents have drifted in quietly to poke around. By now they've checked out just who owns the best water rights in the basin, and they've probably managed to buy some choice property. It could be coincidence Bat Ridley coming up here."

"We know it isn't," Dave Ridley said flatly. "We tracked some of them down into that Flaming Gorge country. Lost them in a thunderstorm. Sooner or later, though, they're goin' to rendezvous with a gunfighter named Jock La Prele. When that happens, Sheriff, we'll know the Clareton brothers' land company is back in operation. And the killings will start again."

The next time Deal Calloway sighted in on the line shack it was to rein away from an exposed ridge. He dug out his field glass, used it to get a better look at some Lonetree waddies unloading supplies from packhorses. Only then did he head on in.

It didn't surprise Deal any that bossman Lon Holter had come up, as Holter, once a top wrangler, knew just how rigorous wintering up here could be. He always brought along the one bottle of corn whiskey to share with his men, along with fetching up news of what had happened in the basin over the winter months. Holter was silver-haired, with a lean and chiseled face. He had a wide smile for Deal Calloway riding up to dismount slowly, but through it questions danced in Holter's light blue eyes.

"A posse tracked up here," Deal said as he reached to shake the other's hand.

He could tell there was a lot more coming out of Deal Calloway, and he drew Deal away from the cowhands packing supplies into the line shack. Holter said, "Cowley, was it?"

"Yup," Deal said reluctantly. "Me and Mort had headed out after the storm had lifted, around noon as I recollect, as we left Cal here as he was ailing some. We just got back too late, Mr. Holter."

"Cal Egan's . . ."

"He was killed by an outlaw named Ridley. I . . . we took Ridley out. It wasn't pretty what he did to Cal."

"Damn," was all Lon Holter could expel through compressed lips. "This storm, we should have been here sooner."

"Mort went down with the posse. He'll take the body, Cal's, for proper burial over to Pitchfork, where Cal grew up."

Deal Calloway didn't remember much of what they discussed last night, the talk divided between how the cattle had fared and their memory of Cal Egan, this, along with nursing that bottle of whiskey. They, he and

39

rancher Lon Holter, had saddled up without partaking of breakfast and caught the downward trail. By mid-morning the sun was out hot and causing a lot of snowmelt.

There should be, in a man cooped up in the confinement of a high mountain line shack, a damned up eagerness to hit into some cow town and really let loose. But Deal felt as empty as corn tassel shucked and tossed away. There was no small talk either between them, just their horses snorting and breathing a little heavier when breaking through a high drift. From what Deal could see snow didn't lay as thick down in the basin, and they were still high enough on Washakie Needles to take in the snow-shrouded Big Horns. It was around midday when Lon Holter reined his bronc off the trail and the short distance to a creek swollen with spring runoff. He set about making a fire, which seemed unusual to Deal Calloway, because generally the rancher preferred a later noon break. Not wanting to interfere with the rancher's thoughts, Deal brought his horse over and let it drink.

"Coffee's hot, Deal."

He nodded at Lon Holter squatting there under limber pines that held back the sunshine. Whereupon he dug a tin cup out of a saddlebag, came near the fire and settled down crosslegged as Holter spilled coffee into the cup he held.

"Last night your shadow did more talking."

Deal worked the first sip of coffee around in his mouth, savoring the harsh chicory taste, then he took another sip while working over in his mind what he wanted to say. "To set the record straight between us,

Lon, it was me gunning down this outlaw. Afterwards . . . that was the hard part. . . ."

The fire, though small, threw out a lot of heat. The rancher stared into the thinning flames, waiting for Deal to continue.

The flames began ebbing lower. Deal Calloway had sunk into the past again, his eyes slitted and filled with just how he'd gunned down that outlaw. Why did he keep emptying his Colt even though he knew the outlaw was dead? It wasn't just Ridley in there, it was Jock La Prele and that damned Englishman, other rawhiders, that he was taking out. They'd not only disfigured him, they had scarred his soul. Once word got out about this, Deal knew his days in the Big Horn Basin were numbered. This time he meant to backtrack deep into Utah and work his way south until he ran out of land or horse.

His glance took in Lon Holter's somber face, and Deal said, "I'll stick around through spring calfing."

"Appreciate that, Deal."

Briefly he detailed what had happened to Cal Egan. "Just between us, Lon, I've seen men killed before, and could have killed a few."

"This Ridley—you knew him from before."

"Could have. But if I hadn't used my gun, someone else would have, Lon."

"You're about the best hand that's ever hooked on at Lonetree. What worries me, worries me a lot, Deal, is that whatever happened to you before is still in there. Worse thing that can happen to any man is holding onto the past. Sometimes it becomes a cancerous sore that won't heal. A man's simply got to let go. Or in a sense he kills himself."

41

"I'll sleep on that, Lon. You're right, though, I've made every day not this day but the past. Now reckon we'd better ride so's we can hit the home buildings before sundown."

Three

They were busted and out of grub and damning Pike Gear for holding them on this wind-lashed rise some two miles north of the Birdseye stage station. Red gritty dust stung at their faces and blurred their vision of the stagecoach trail cutting their way. Below in a dry wash to the north their horses held amongst dry brush. Behind them, maybe four miles, that jagged cut separating the Owl Creek and Bridger mountains was Wind River Canyon. The river of the same name passed through it, and beyond that lay Old Thermopolis and its welcoming hot springs, where'd they be right now had not Gear decided the stagecoach would be easy pickings.

Soddy Kling, in a pissed-off undertone, muttered to the outlaw folded down next to him, "I've done some stupid things in my life . . . but chokin' out here on this dust . . ."

"I know. La Prele promised we'd be paid once we hit into . . . what the hell's the name of that town . . ."

"Old Thermopolis."

"But I ain't about to buck Pike—not with that short temper of his, and Pike nursin' them boils."

43

Mirthless laughter bubbled out of Soddy Kling, blinking gritty sand out of his eyes as a gust of wind just about tore his hat away. He was gun crazy, with two sixguns strapped around his waist, a Derringer in a holster strapped around his left shin, another stored in a saddlebag, and the Remington in his saddle booth. He was itching to get on with it, get up in the Big Horn Basin, where according to Jock La Prele, it would start again.

The other one, Frank Hutto, was a nondescript man in worn clothing. If someone said throw down on a woman or child, he'd do it; all Hutto cared about was getting paid. The walrus mustache hid his down-drooping mouth, and from him came the vague stench of garlic, which he preferred to a chaw of tobacco. He took a lazy glance over at Pike Gear, who was snoozing under what shade a small bush offered, on his side so's to ease the pain emanating from his buttock.

Hutto muttered, "Pike can smell money. Anyway, I don't want to hit up there busted either, in case La Prele shows up late."

Sipping from his canteen, Kling said, "About run out of water too, dammit."

"Wind River's yonder."

"Ah, to hell with it." He shoved the cork back into his canteen. Pushing to his knees, he peered southerly and grimaced at the plume of dust rising on the stagecoach road. "Might be that coach."

Shoving up, Hutto said, "About time. Yup, I can make it out two on top. Hey, Pike, here she comes."

Lifting his hat from his face, Pike Gear cast an owly glance at the others. He was solid through the shoulders and midriff, with thick black brows on a wide

44

face. He wore a dark brown vest over a plain shirt, and the one gun. He just hated the thought of easing into a saddle again. What had La Prele said, he groused, about there being these mineral springs up there, at Old Thermopolis? Sourly he threw at them, "Well, get the hosses."

As Hutto and Kling came down the slope to the wash, Pike Gear got up slowly. One look to the south revealed the stagecoach was being held to a walk up the long slanting lay of land between Gear and Birdseye stage station. Gear knew the stagecoach was heading for the same destination, which meant they couldn't leave any witnesses behind. He was also disregarding orders from La Prele that they ease quietly into the Big Horn Basin.

"Let Jock take care of hisself. Any women aboard that coach, Hutto will like that."

Pike Gear didn't feel any qualms about what was to happen, he judged, within a half-hour, or about the bloody events that had taken place down in Colorado. He had enough problems of his own, between these lousy boils and trying to avoid running into any lawmen. He surveyed the wide sweep of land running down to the stage station and easterly through cynical eyes.

"A good place to start a graveyard."

Ever since stagecoaching out of Casper, Justin Blaine had been hungering for a glimpse of the approaches to the Big Horn Basin. Part of the banker's thoughts were worries about his Oklahoma City bank. Mostly though, it was about Cleo. He had been separated from her, going on a year, and now he had to convince her to leave all of this to the law and come back home.

The first part of his long journey had been somewhat comfortable, by train all the way to Denver, and to Casper, now the dusty-jarring rigors of this stagecoach. He wore a black suit that was flecked with dust, and he was square of face and of frame, with pleasant features. His traveling companions were a carpetbagger huddled asleep next to him, and opposite, a bland-faced man rigged out in a rumpled brown suit and the coat open to show the gun belt, and a halfblood clad in the working garb of a cowhand. The halfblood had gotten on at the stage station, his cold black eyes telling everyone else to leave him the hell alone with any white man's talk. His name was Osage Mattson, and he was on his way to Greybull and the T-C ranch.

Justin Blaine still hadn't figured out the makeup of the bland-faced man, only that somehow he'd come up with another bottle of whiskey after they'd left the stage station, and had gotten on at Casper. Somehow this Slater Green, even with that gun belt strapped around his waist, didn't look as threatening as the halfblood, and he'd proved to be a talker. Now he started up again.

"So, Mr. Blaine, I ain't been up in the Big Horn Basin either. Hope it ain't as forlorn as the places we've staged through; so far a hundred some miles of nothing but jackrabbits, pronghorns, and dust."

"God created all of this. I believe these pronghorns are actually antelope—an interesting species."

"Bony as hell when you butcher one up. You don't do it within the first hour or so the carcass begins to stink up. I like elk myself."

46

"I've heard they are difficult to hunt. No, no whiskey, thank you."

Through the window at his left elbow Slater Green peered ahead at a mountain range they'd have to cross over. Up there, he figured, if the opportunity ever presented itself, he could lift this Oklahoman's big fat wallet.

Before turning to the more adventurous life of being a gunhand Green had been a pickpocket, in New Orleans, and places further westerly. He still had some money from a mugging he'd done just before entraining out of Cheyenne. Swigging from the bottle, he let it build in him, though it didn't show on his face, this scorn he felt for high-minded folks such as Justin Blaine. Pronghorn, antelope, who in tarnation cared what they called that prairie critter.

In a voice tempered with a smile Slater Green said as he swilled the whiskey around in the bottle, "You ever been down to El Paso? Anyway, Mr. Blaine, down in that Texas town they call this brew Pass Whiskey. You ever heard of tangleleg?"

"I'm sorry, I . . ."

"Whiskey," he snickered. "Goes down smooth as barbed wire tickling your Adam's apple. Taos lightning, valley tan, forty-rod—whiskey, different names in different places. But this corn mash I'm drinking now"—he shrugged—"tastes like tarantula piss." Laughing, he settled in deeper on the seat, with the halfblood holding his stare out the window in the door.

Up where he sat with the reins wrapped in his liver-speckled hands, Dutch Trajon knew that once he pulled into Old Thermopolis it would be the end of the line for him as a stagecoach driver. He didn't want it this way, but the new owner felt that at sixty Trajon just couldn't cut it. What had helped on this last run was the presence of shotgun Tom Diehl. They were about out of words, at least Dutch Trajon was, worry settling in for what the future held. He hadn't saved all that much toward retirement.

They were going up a long grade. The trail was fairly straight, and beyond this stretched a low swale of barren prairie extending to the Bridgers. Blinking dust out of his eyes, Trajon said, "Reckon I'll even miss a dusty day like this, Tom."

"Don't you have family back East?"

"A sister, in Pittsburgh. If she's still alive. We Trajons just don't keep in touch. We . . ."

A strangled cry of pain came from Tom Diehl, and the next thing Trajon realized his seat companion had sagged down. It was all Trajon could do to control the horses reacting to the reverberating echo of a rifle, then someone called out, "Rein up, old-timer, or you're a dead man!" Somehow Trajon held the horses on the road, though the leaders had swung to the left, and with one of them bucking up when a horseman appeared.

Gripping a sixgun, Pike Gear yelled, "Vacate that coach or we'll open up." Shifting in the saddle to ease the pain springing away from his left buttock, he took note of his two saddlemates coming out of concealment and in on the coach. Gear yelled again as he punched a slug into the top of the door frame, "The next one is gonna punch a hole in someone's fat belly!"

The first to emerge was the halfblood, but cautiously, and his arms uplifted. Then Justin Blaine got out and stepped back to stand alongside Osage Mattson, not sure what to do. Inside the coach the carpetbagger had been roused by the sound of the rifle, with him focusing in on the other occupant of the coach smiling at the sight of Pike Gear.

Now Slater Green called out, "Hey, Pike, its me, Slater. I'm coming out." Rising into a crouch, he forced the carpetbagger up from the seat, then he shoved the man out the open door. As the carpetbagger tumbled to the ground, Slater Green crouched outside, laughing.

Frank Hutto waved a greeting as he brought his horse around the back of the coach and trained his rifle on the men standing there. "In that suit, Slater, you look like an undertaker. How you been?"

"I still ain't wound up in no jail."

"Cut the bullcrap, Slater," groused Pike Gear, "and disarm these men."

A scorning glance took Slater Green past the carpetbagger. He spat out to the halfblood, "Just keep those arms up. Turn around now, slowly, and brace against the wheel." The wind clawed around the outlaw as he brought a cautious hand in to claim Osage Mattson's sixgun and the big hunting knife. The others had turned around to face the coach, and he pawed through the banker's clothing, coming up with a leather wallet and a gold watch and gold chain that had a couple of garnets set in it. Clutching his booty in one hand, he smiled at the carpetbagger holding out his wallet and some loose bills.

Pike Gear motioned the driver off the high seat, and when Trajon had labored down he was told to stand with the others. By now Soddy Kling had reined in holding onto his Winchester. He held out about ten yards, as had Frank Hutto, picking at his nose as Gear called out his name.

49

"Frank, get up there and latch onto them reins. Then throw down the strongbox." Gear glanced southward down the stagecoach road, into the angling wind, checking for a dusty sign of anyone pulling this way out of the stage station. The road seemed clear, and he looked back at the men he was about to order killed. When the strongbox pitched down by the front wheel, he let out a satisfied grunt.

"Please," stammered the carpetbagger, "you have all of our worldly possessions, just let . . ."

Osage Mattson threw the man a lidded glance. He knew the slightest wrong word would see them all killed. Before him there was nothing but sagebrush littering the open prairie and the barren road, and to break that way would be like a seven ball spinning across a pool table but finding no pocket to drop into. The one doing all the talking, this Pike Gear, was a bad hombre. Or maybe it was just that sun-bloated face registering some inner discomfort. An order from Slater Green brought the halfblood and his companions turning away from the coach.

When Pike Gear called out, "You got a good grip on them reins, Hutto?", the halfblood knew leaden slugs were about to come singing his way.

And even as Osage Mattson spun to his right in an attempt to get around the stagecoach and maybe below that downcrop of land further along the road, he staggered under the impact of slugs penetrating into his thigh and side. He folded down quickly, not moving, through the haze of shock and sudden pain.

At a crouch Slater Green was laughing and blazing away with a pair of sixguns, one of them the halfblood's. Pike Gear's sixgun was bucking in his hand, while

Soddy Kling was levering and pumping shells at the three others crumbling down. A slug danced the coach door shut, the side of the coach was crisscrossed with bullet holes, and dust spurted up where more shells hit into the ground. The noise of their guns was a comforting staccato of killing to these rawhiders. While Frank Hutto was having a rough go of it holding in the horses.

The shooting stopped, then Soddy Kling's rifle barked, and he had a satisfied smirk for the bullet finding the banker's gaping left eye. "Dumb shit," growled Pike Gear, as he brought his horse in closer while dropping loads into the cylinder of his sixgun. He took in the bullet-torn and bloody bodies, took note of the fact that not all that many bullets had struck into the halfblood. A quick snap shot struck in near Osage Mattson's left ear, and when the halfblood didn't stir, Gear swung down and ground-hitched his reins.

"Well, you two, load them bodies into the coach while I break open the strongbox."

"What the hell, Pike, just leave them here—"

"Then we pass around them mountains and show up in Old Thermopolis spending money like there's no t'morrow. Load 'em up, then we'll dump this coach over by the Wind River someplace." He took a step, paused, and snarled, "Damn these boils; there's gotta be a sawbones up there."

His sixgun belched flame and the lock on the strongbox broke open. Holstering his weapon, Gear crouched down slowly, removed the lock and opened the strongbox. In it was a couple of money bags, one addressed to some bank in Old Thermopolis, the other unmarked, and he emptied the contents of both bags on the ground. Plus the weapons and money and personal effects taken from the passengers, and he expected Frank Hutto had emptied out the shotgun's pockets, their killing wages from the strongbox came to around three thousand dollars. "Could have been worse—could have come up with some rocks or road apples."

The bodies were dumped back into the coach, and then the strongbox. Slater Green piled aboard Hutto's horse, and with Pike out front they continued north along the road until they reached some rocky ground stretching out along a wash toward the Wind River, by Pike's estimation no more than a mile or more away.

Elation rode with Slater Green. He'd held back to come in behind the stagecoach, to find in one of the carpetbagger's valises several bottles of whiskey wrapped in cotton batting to prevent them from jostling together and breaking. His pleased yell resounded up to Pike Gear slouched in his saddle, and to Kling on the other side of the coach. As Kling eased his horse back, a bottle looped toward him, and somehow he caught it. Then Green was pulling up by the front wheel to toss a bottle up to Hutto. He loped ahead to come in alongside Gear and handed the man a bottle, while Gear muttered, "That's right, all we need to do right now is get so whiskeyed up we can't ride."

"Aw, shit, Pike, ease off," said Slater Green.

"Just don't guzzle that stuff down like its spring water. Tonight, when we're out around them mountains someplace, you can drink yo'self into a stupor. Where the hell did you get that suit?"

"It do make me look kind of dignified."

"More like someone about ready to take up permanent residence in a pine box. That shotgun only took the one slug; when we get up by the river take what he's wearing."

"Won't be the first time I wore a dead man's boots."

"Knowing you, probably won't be the last."

What brought Osage Mattson out of the deep pit of darkness and pain was a rustling sound. Now that he'd sorted it out it was kind of like the frantic beating of the wings of Canadian geese trying to skim out from under the guns of hunters. But instead of the deep-throated honking of geese, the halfblood knew he was in the midst of turkey vultures squabbling away and tearing at naked flesh.

This thought came: *must have been stirring about, must have known I was alive, or they'd have swarmed over me.* And now one did, to a beating of wings and a waddling walk, as it fluttered over the halfblood and pushed in to where the others lay.

The halfblood began heaving and gaping open his mouth to spill out the contents of his stomach through caked lips. When he licked blood away, he remembered he'd been hit more than once. That he was still alive told him that, though he was pierced with bullets, no vital organs had been damaged. His hat was gone, and he hoped back up on the stagecoach road where somebody might come upon it. Focusing more, he could make out glinting water, weeds, the smell of the river, and mud caking his face.

It came to him, slowly, the jostling motion of the coach as it trekked over rough ground, of his being stretched out over other bodies, and one draped over him, then everything fading away. Dimly he could make out, began to realize, the other passengers were lying just on this side of the stagecoach silhouetted by starlight. White man's cruelty! Those killers could have left the bodies inside the coach. But no, their cruel nature had caused them to dump the bodies out here where the carrion could get at them better. Maybe these killers were still lurking nearby just to watch creatures as low as them pick out eyes and tongues and render flesh into bloody strips.

He groaned through gritted teeth when he realized his left hipbone had been shattered. Osage Mattson considered himself to be tough as they came, the realization settling in that he was going to find out if he could live up to his expectations.

"River . . . must drink . . ."

He stretched out his arms, dug in with right leg, and thrust himself forward, a bare couple of inches, and when he did, the carrion rose in mass confusion. Under him the mud was cooling, gripping at him as he poked ahead on his belly to the first traces of water. That dark object? A log, which he reached out for, to pull himself free from the clutching mud. And then he was floating while holding onto a barren tree branch. He took in a mouthful of water, managed to swallow some of it, barely awake but doggedly hanging to his awareness of that. Osage Mattson knew that if he passed out again the river would claim his body.

With the water touching his wounds, he set about getting his bearings. As there was no crossing, he figured he was still east of the river and not all that far from the road. They could have unharnessed the horses and taken them along in hopes of selling them. The Birdseye stage station, and how to get there. Instinct told the halfblood to hold along the river, to work his way south. As for the here and now, there came another memory jog.

"That carpetbagger was . . . peddling whiskey."

Pulling himself into the bank, it suddenly came to him that part of his pain came from the left side of his head. Reaching there, he found that the back part of his ear had been shot away and an ugly furrow traced up through his shaggy black hair. He was never a man to use cuss words, even when riled up considerable. But now as his anger grew over what these men had done to him, Osage Mattson let go with some ugly verbiage, which quickly died away. For he knew such things were only a waste of time.

Now he began the ordeal of reaching the coach, not only for the whiskey, but for something to plug his wounds, and find a weapon that had been overlooked. Painfully he worked on his belly toward the back of the coach, pausing when the pain became unbearable, picking up the sound of water splashing as a fish jumped or the steady croaking of frogs. The halfblood realized he was there when his groping hand touched the back wheel. He used both hands to pull himself closer, rested awhile, and then he managed to get to his feet.

He sagged against the boot where merchandise and pieces of luggage were lashed down. He found one valise that had been opened and was empty, and by it another, which he managed to pry open, with his hand dipping inside to come into contact with something shaped like a bottle of whiskey. He felt himself dropping down. But he fought the weakness of the moment as he brought the bottle to his mouth and wrapped his teeth around the cork to pop it free. He drank deeply, gasped at the shock of so much whiskey hitting into his empty belly. But as the warmth of the whiskey spread, he could feel it taking hold to chase away a lot of pain.

Lifting his eyes, he could make out some swooping forms, and a bitter snarl for the vultures ripped out of his mouth. Now he worked around the coach to the door which sagged open. Folding his upper body into the coach, he pulled up and in, on his belly, then he worked onto his good hip and managed to prop his back against the other door. He'd spilled some whiskey, but the bottle was still half-full.

Osage Mattson knew he'd lost a lot of blood, and that a couple of slugs were still in him. He gulped down some more whiskey, as through the open door he could make out turkey vultures swooping down. It was getting colder too, he suddenly realized. If it dropped below the freezing mark, in these wet clothes he stood every chance of freezing to death. At this thought a smile cut an uncaring line across his face. He knew that if the cold didn't finish the job these killers had started, the wounds eating at his body would. A good sign, in Osage Mattson's opinion, would be if he opened his eyes in the morning and caught a glimpse of sunlight, but that was hours away, and he still had some whiskey to drink. He raised the bottle to his lips.

Then he said just before passing out, "Donkey piss has got more kick."

Four

Washakie Needles rose some thirteen thousand feet, looming over the lesser Owl Creek range casting shadows down upon the Wind River and some horses belonging to McBean & Company's Middle Fork Express. After being turned loose, they'd broken away and then banded back together to come in further north along the river, burdened down with harnesses and the bits still in their mouths. They wouldn't drift far, as they'd gotten accustomed to having hay and oats brought to them, but they were still spooked by all that gunfire.

This mountain, Washakie Needles, was the southernmost arm of the Absarokas. Back near its summit, sunlight webbed through wind-flung snow. Though the snow had patched out in the foothills, Deal Calloway and rancher Lon Holter had found it tough going since pulling out of the line shack. They still had to come down through a narrow canyon in the foothills, which opened up to Holter jogging ahead to the scent of pine wafting away from junipers. In amongst the trees it was darker, but they gave a certain comfort to Lon Holter, for it meant they were nearly to the home buildings. In

57

gaps through the trees, while his horse walked along the winding trail, Holter was still high enough to see way down into the floor of the basin.

He was luckier than others in that his father had come in during the '70's to begin building up the ranch. There were a lot of dealings with the Crow, these Indians having been driven out of the Powder River area by the Sioux. Now the Crow had settled up north and east of the Big Horns, and ever since taking over after his father had passed away, Holter had built up Lonetree into an outfit that needed a dozen or so waddies in the peak summer months.

Lon Holter had come to know what he was viewing in the dying light of day as a huge basin, in Western parlance a hole, a valley more or less completely surrounded by mountains. It was an area so spacious that in the middle of it the mountains were more or less invisible. Down south of his spread was what everyone called the back door into the Big Horn Basin. Some came into it on horseback through the Wind River Canyon. The stageline road swung easterly around the Bridgers.

Except for the semidesert terrain alongside and above the Big Horn River valley, all of the good ranching country was deeded. A rancher hung on as long as he could, so it got so that there were a lot of longtime neighbors. As he gazed yonderly, Lon Holter's concern over the killing of one of his hands was pushed aside by his worry that change was coming to the basin. He'd been made aware of this on a trip over to Meeteetse to stock up on supplies. Some old-time ranchers were selling out. He knew that some of them, Tom Evans and Hank Houx, were having money problems, and could understand their wanting to sell. But other names had been brought up. Hugh DeTell, for instance, among the first to settle into the basin. Much of this had happened last summer, when land agents had come in. Now it was spring, and the land agents were back.

Change: it was something that Lon Holter hadn't seen too much of in the basin. Its very isolation had kept change out. He liked it this way, this splendid isolation that kept out a lot of lawbreakers. His biggest concern was that part of what he'd heard was of these land agents only buying land along waterways, and of there being some violence last summer. But nothing to issue a warrant over.

His attention was drawn to a log fence which extended out from the main buildings, and to some of his horses that were swinging to look at the incoming riders. The fence ran back to hook up with the canyon wall, and in it would be the summer remuda. Before he'd put up the fence, the horses roamed freely, and sometimes too far so that it took a lot of morning to round them up. As the back of a tack house loomed out of the lowering trees, he slowed up some to have Deal Calloway come alongside.

He said, "Marge wants you to have supper with us at the main house."

"There's a woman I can never disappoint."

"Asides, Deal, she's prepared your favorite, southern fried chicken. About Egan, I'll break the news to Marge after supper is over. As Marge is all a'fluttery over one of our daughters expecting at any time."

"That'll be Diana over at Old Thermopolis."

"I expect we'll be headin' over there tomorrow. I'd sure admire you coming along. Afterwards it'll be another ride up to Meeteetse to make arrangements for Egan's funeral."

Deal Calloway exchanged tired glances with the rancher and he said, "Ground frozen as it is, it'll be at least a month before they can bury Egan. All the same, I won't miss the funeral."

"Marge, I expect she'll hang on at Old Thermopolis to take care of the baby until Diana is up and around. Yeah, Cal Egan, if that storm hadn't hit . . ."

They rode around the tack house and toward log buildings and a long, low log house, the buildings hemmed in by junipers and the narrow canyon walls, the creek where the trail to town curled northeasterly rushing and boiling over small boulders. All of the buildings were stained a dark brown and were tidy, and into a barn they brought their horses as a collie came bounding after them.

By lanternlight they took in waddy Tubby Green using a pitchfork to spread out straw in the stalls occupied by a few horses. As the collie leaped up to be petted by Holter, the waddy said, "Howdy, Deal, Mr. Holter. Figured you'd be back around sundown, with the snow and all. I'll take care of your hosses."

"We had any visitors since I was gone?"

"Just the vet coming out to check over the horses. And one or two drifters, cowhands lookin' to hook on someplace for the summer."

"Anyone worth hiring?"

"Yup, Nat Miller."

This provoked from Lon Holter a curious squinting of his eyes. "Nat's a fixture with the T-C outfit."

"That outfit is being sold, according to Nat."

Throwing a glance at Deal Calloway, the rancher

said sharply, "I find that hard to swallow. Just doesn't fit to what I know of Clement Bryant." He got to thinking about those land buyers again, and left it there. The long ride back here had tuckered the pair of them out, and so had their concern over the violence back up on Washakie Needles. They left the barn, with Deal detouring over to the bunkhouse to wash up and change clothes. The rancher and the collie took the longer walk over barren ground to the main house that looked as if it had been here longer than a lot of these trees.

Rancher Lon Holter wouldn't have it any other way but that they head over to the fireplace to partake of some sipping brandy. Knowing the rancher wasn't as prone to drinking as he was, Deal realized that Holter was still troubled over what had happened up at the line shack.

During supper, Marge Holter had brightened things up with her presence and gentle smile. Now she was in the kitchen helping the cook clean up things. The house was big enough to have a separate dining room used to feed the hired hands, and where Deal sat he gazed about at the momentos Holter had collected over the years. In Deal was a suppressed envy for what the rancher had—holdings, but more than that, a good woman. His boots on a large, circular throw rug on the hardwood floor, the fire warmly embracing and the only light in the main living room, he took the glass of brandy from the rancher settling down in a chair. Both of them were facing the fireplace.

"I sure wish you'd change your mind."

"I'll be quitting the best job I ever had, Lon. I hate

to think on it. You know how it is, when word gets around."

"You had to kill the outlaw, Deal. It had to be done. After what he did to Cal Egan, if not you it would have been someone else."

"Guess I was in the wrong place at the wrong time."

Holter nodded absently, his boots off and his legs stretched out to show his woolen socks. The talk turned to spring calfing and what another cold spell could do to newborn calves. Deal knew Holter was building up to something, as by now they'd worked the bottle down a little, and Holter had gotten up once to throw another log into the fireplace.

"Nat . . . Nat Miller, up and quitting the T-C. Can't figure that one. Unless . . ." He set his glass on a coffee table. "It started last summer, Deal. Now, this spring, when I went over to Meeteetse, I hear some of them are back."

"I don't follow your drift, Lon."

"Oh, you don't get into town all that much. I should have checked it out at the land office when I was in Meeteetse. But I just wanted to get back and bring some supplies up to the line shack. Anyway, Deal, what's afoot is that men I've known for most of my life are selling out."

"The T-C?"

"That one's a puzzler. They're back, but not as bunchy as last summer, some land agents, Deal. Buying up whatever land they can."

Now it was Deal Calloway setting his glass aside. His face had gone wooden. The camaraderie of a moment ago bended away, and a face out of the past ghosted in to dance in the glow of light over the fireplace. That was Bat Ridley he'd just killed. Ridley's presence meant the others were gathering, and if not in the basin, were on the way. All the more reason for him to cut out of the basin, cut out now before he got involved in this.

"You okay, Deal?"

"Yeah, I . . . guess its just too much brandy."

"That's right, you're not all that much a drinker. But tonight I needed a bracer." Consulting his watch, Holter added, "Late, going on eleven."

Deal came to his feet and said, "Tell Marge I'm obliged for that wonderful meal."

"I hope you figure on going with us to Old Thermopolis tomorrow."

"Yeah, I'll sleep on it. G'night, Lon."

Even when they were a long ways past Grass Creek and had crossed an arm of the Big Horn River, Deal Calloway hadn't sorted out all of his reasons for tagging along. Some of it was of his loyalty to the Holters. Also, he hadn't set foot in a cow town since winter had set in last year. Once he'd enjoyed the feel of a deck of cards, and the attentions of a woman. He'd discarded these habits ever since pulling out of Colorado.

Why had he gone along to Old Thermopolis? Last night had been an emotional tug-of-war. Instead of finding his bunk, he'd gone on to sort out how he felt by the creek. Just Ridley by himself didn't mean all that much. If the old bunch of rawhiders was gathering, the Clareton brothers were behind it. They'd come in to the basin through the back door, which meant to probably rendezvous at the town Deal Calloway would reach in a couple of hours.

"Deal?"

The voice of Marge Holter distracted his thoughts. He reined in closer to ride alongside the buggy, and she said, "Lon told me you might be pulling out."

"I just might, Mrs. Holter."

"You'll be sorely missed. No matter what they say about what happened up there, I would have done the same thing. Egan was too young to have this happen."

Lon Holter said as he nodded to a shading grove of aspens, "I could use some of those sandwiches Marge packed along. And some Arbuckles."

It would be hard, Deal realized, to pull out of here. As he probably would never work for a better man than Lon Holter. It could be he was running from the past just as much as the past seemed to be catching up with him. Coming in under the trees, he got down slowly, with his eyes slanting easterly at the Big Horns hazed by sunlight and the rising heat of day. He'd found out there was a certain comfort in viewing something that man hadn't yet conquered, nor ever would. Now as he examined his thoughts, Deal knew he wouldn't accomplish anything by drawing that final paycheck. Somehow he had to conquer his uncertainties, too. They owed him, not so much for the scar blemishing his face, but in a sense for making him less of a man.

Turning, he looked at Holter stooping as he collected firewood, and Deal headed that way. A glance leftward revealed Marge Holter preoccupied in spreading out a blanket on a patch of browned grass. "Lon," he said tentatively, "there's somethin' you ought to know. These land agents . . . they could be part of what happened down in Colorado a few years back."

Five

The road from the north cut in close to a roof-topped, dark-red mesa, and when the road plunged sharply, Deal Calloway regarded the ramshackle buildings placed randomly up and down hills surrounding Old Thermopolis. At the base of the mesa and below the road a single hot, bubbling green pool threw water over large terraces dropping one by one toward the Big Horn River. At the southern end of this thermal spring he took in a line of log bathing establishments.

He'd fallen behind a little, and now he jogged his bronc after the rancher's buggy picking up speed on the downward sloping road. During his winter sojourn up at the line shack he'd let his hair grow shaggy enough so that it touched upon his shoulders. On windy days the hair covered some of the facial burn mark. But today, as was generally the case in this part of the basin, the air was calm and had in it the smell of an early spring. He could use some nicer weather, and more importantly, seek to ease some of his body aches in that thermal spring. He stated his intentions to Lon Holter, who said, "Wish I could join you, Deal. But we're anxious to get on to my daughter's; her house is the other side of that little knob of hill. She'll put me and Sarah up. Take my room at the Chandler Hotel—they'll bill me for your expenses."

"I'm obliged for that, Lon."

"The least I can do." He threw Deal a wave, and then reined away from the main road for what passed for a street cutting away to the west.

Pressing on, Deal passed along a wide boulevard he'd traversed once before, this when finding his searching way into the basin. A median with dun-colored grass separated the street lined by old stone buildings. Others were wood-framed, either crowded in close or with an empty lot to either side. For a weekday a lot of horses were tied to hitching racks. Other business places were set along side streets, and should be, since this cow town was the county seat of Hot Springs County.

A big white sign bordered in black brought Deal another half-block to the Chandler Hotel. It was two-storied, the stone wall stuccoed a glaring white, and flat-roofed, and kind of remindful of a hotel he'd stayed at down in Tucson. When he eased out of the saddle, a lad of around twelve burst out of the hotel and grinned his way across the boardwalk.

"You checking in, mister?"

"Yup."

"Stable your horse?"

"Whereabouts?"

"Kitty-corner across the block. Albers Livery stable."

"How much?"

"I generally charge a dime." The boy began to notice the tall cowhand's disfigured face, but when Deal fingered out a quarter, the boy stopped edging away.

"Two bits if the job is done right." He handed the reins over, then Deal turned around and untied his saddlebags and bedroll. A sudden smile from Deal sealed the bargain, along with bringing one in return. "By the way, what does that stable charge?"

"A buck a day, mister."

"You get any commission off that—"

"What's commission?"

"What makes this world go round. Tell that hostler to give my hoss a good rubdown." He swung away to tramp across the boardwalk and find the lobby.

Where he said to the clerk, "Mr. Holter sent me over."

"Certainly."

"That I'm to take his room."

"Just sign the register. The thermal spring? Ah, Mr. Calloway, we cart water from the spring over here. For the convenience of our guests."

"Have these taken to my room. First I'll need some clothes from that mercantile store." While signing in, he'd taken notice of the names in the register, found none that he remembered from the past. And in coming into the lobby of the few cattlemen milling about and through the open door leading into the barroom and of more of them idling over drinks at the bar or huddled around tables playing cards. He couldn't make out any of them as being cowhands. Perhaps they were in town for some county meeting. Some of them he'd recognized, but left it at that as he turned to head out the front door.

Deal Calloway was just another cowpuncher to the four riders closing in on the Chandler Hotel. By the time Pike Gear had come in to heave out of the saddle, Deal had gone into the mercantile store, and Gear, gripped with discomfort and in a sour mood, rasped out to Frank Hutto, "This is it, the Chandler Hotel."

"What name did La Prele say he'd be using?"

"Just like you to forget."

Slater Green went up on the boardwalk as if he meant to go into the hotel, but then Gear was grabbing at his arm to swing Green around, and Pike Gear said, "La Prele wants us to stay clear of this hotel, savvy?"

Smiling away his anger at what Gear had done, Slater Green said, "Must mean that those Englishmen are gonna be bunkin' here too. No sweat, as there's a couple of more hotels upstreet." He watched Pike Gear tramp into the hotel, then he stepped down and began untying his reins from the hitchrack. Hutto and Soddy Kling hadn't bothered to dismount.

"I hate bein' around Pike when he's like this."

"Why the hell doesn't he find a doctor?"

"He don't like bein' cut."

Climbing into the saddle, Slater Green said, "Then let the damned fool suffer."

Hutto said, "I thought for a second you was gonna brace Pike."

"Would you have?" Slater Green threw back, and when Hutto didn't come back, Green laughed as he swung his horse around. "I'll get us some rooms at that hotel yonder."

In the lobby, Pike Gear wasn't sure what to make of all the cattlemen milling about. Now there were two clerks on duty, and he directed a question at an older man with sallow features. "Did Sam Morgan check in yet?"

"I'm not sure."

The other clerk said, "We're holding some rooms for Mr. Morgan. Fortunately he wired some money up, otherwise . . ." His eyes slid to the occupants of the lobby. "Ah, he was expected to show up yesterday."

"He'll show," snapped Pike Gear. Only the fact people were bunched in close to the counter kept him from throwing some cuss words at the clerk, chiefly because here he was in Old Thermopolis and La Prele and the others weren't here. More than this, he needed something to ease the dull ache emanating from his buttocks. Just the thought of having those boils lanced caused his teeth to grit together. At a slow walk he came out of the lobby to survey the business places on Main Street. Only when he came across the boardwalk did he realize that Slater Green was gone.

And Soddy Kling muttered, "Slater took off to find us some rooms; over there, the Archer Hotel."

Gear, deciding not to try the rigors of getting back into the saddle, brought his horse at a tired walk after Hutto and Kling, who were reining away and angling upstairs, and the pair of blocks that would fetch them in alongside Slater Green's trail-worn horse hitched before the hotel. Coming through an intersection, Pike Gear took in other business places on an eastward-running street, among them the office of Doc Tack Youmans.

"Damn, there's a sawbones . . . but . . . damn . . ." He kept trudging on toward the hotel, not all that eager to go under a doctor's knife, and damning Jock La Prele and the weather in general.

* * *

They could feel it coming in, an upthrust of warming wind that had arisen over the Absarokas and down-drafted into the basin, to chase the chill of early night away from the town. The cattlemen who'd crowded into town knew that if this kept up, come sunup the creeks would be spilling a lot of snowmelt into the Big Horn River. And though it might cause cows heavy with calf to give early birth, still they welcomed the weather change.

As he'd promised, Lon Holter had hooked up with Deal Calloway in the barroom at the Chandler Hotel. The first topic of discussion was that his daughter wasn't due to have her baby for another week at least. Along with this, Holter was happy to exchange greetings with a lot of old friends. He'd found Deal facing away from the back end of the bar, but with an elbow hooked on it. Calloway was watching a nearby poker game. One thing that rancher had taken pains to check on when coming into the barroom if there were any sidelong glances or small talk concerning Deal Calloway. There hadn't been, and Holter knew word still hadn't gotten out about that shooting up on Washakie Needles. Now over a bottle of whiskey they were debating where to have supper just as Jimbo Rood, the segundo for the Pitchfork Ranch, sidled up to order a round.

"Obliged," Holter said as he returned Rood's smile.

"Did I hear someone mention chowin' down at Mustang Mae's—"

"I was torn between that," Holter confessed, "and samplin' the vittles over at Chubby Dexter's."

"Are they still on the outs?"

"You know Mae, you get on her bad side don't bother goin' over to her place. Last I heard, Lon, Mustang Mae and Chubby have threated to go at one another with guns."

"An' all because," Holter shook his head, "Chubby claimed he made a tastier apple pie."

Jimbo Rood, with a smile that included Deal, said, "As I recollect, Chubby's words were more like that road apples tasted better than the pies Mae put out. So Mae does have public opinion on her side."

"Along with that temper of hers." Lon Holter picked one of his silver dollars up from the bar and flipped it into the air, and said as he reached to catch the spinning coin, "You call it, Deal."

"Heads."

"Heads it is. Means we're headin' over to Mustang Mae's. Jimbo, I'm springin' for supper if you want to tag along."

They left the hotel, where Rood informed them that he was in here representing the interests of the Pitchfork Ranch at this county meeting. And Holter said, "Otto Franc likes to stay close to home during spring calfing." Franc's real full name was Count Otto Franc von Lichtenstein, one of the great cattle ranchers in the basin. Over the years Holter and Franc had hunted a lot of big game together, and since their ranches adjoined one another, they'd gotten together for family affairs. The way its warming up, mused Holter, he knew he should have stayed home too. But he also knew that part of being a grandfather was to share in the worries of childbirth.

"Lon, Mr. Franc wants to hold a meeting over at Meeteetse. He's worried about what's been happening, some old-time ranchers up and selling out."

"He shares my concern, Jimbo. Especially since we've

had good weather the last few years and most everyone is stocked up on more cattle." It seemed more logical to Lon Holter for Franc to have held this meeting at Pitchfork, a small waystop of a cow town fringing on the eastern limits of his land. Then again, Holter knew there were some smaller ranchers that would never set foot in Pitchfork but just might show up at Meeteetse. These men were proud and independent, a mite clannish about who they called friend—traits that Lon Holter knew cut to the bone to just about describe him, and Jimbo Rood for that matter, no matter that Rood had drifted down from Montana—lordy, could it be going on fifteen years now?

Coming onto a wood-framed building with a peaked roof, he glanced Rood's way. The segundo was a little heftier, looked youngish despite those lines creasing along his mouth, but now he noticed the threads of grey hair along Jimbo Rood's temple. Holter knew he'd changed too. It took longer in the morning to get going. Unlike the Pitchfork Ranch, he couldn't afford the luxury of taking on a foreman. Now with the three daughters he'd sired married and gone, and no son to take over, him edged past the sixty mark, it came down to just how much longer he wanted to keep ranching. Marge had been harping at him to sell out and come in here to Old Thermopolis so's to be closer to some of their grandchildren. If anything he preferred Meeteetse, but to retire meant a change to a new kind of life that just might see him pine away into an early grave.

He came in behind the others, into Mustang Mae's boxlike cafe, where no frilly curtains held along the window, and the tables were covered with checkered red and white cloth Mae had purchased over at Avery's

Mercantile Store. The place was crowded, and noisy, and as usual Mae was snapping at one of her waitresses to get the lead out and serve the customers. There was one empty table, which Jimbo Rood claimed, Deal and Lon Holter pulling chairs away to ease down as Mustang Mae's hoarsy whistle cut through the chatter.

The three of them smiled at Mae barking out now, "Jimbo, how the hell are they hanging. And howdy too there Lon Holter." She came out of the kitchen wiping her hands on a grease-stained apron, a big woman wearing trousers and boots and a floppy shirt that was rolled up to her elbows. The hat was a relic to when Mae ran her own freighting outfit. Her hair was snarly and pinned up under the hat, and her age showed in her oval face, and it was her smiling luminous brown eyes that held Deal Calloway's as she surveyed him.

"Who the hell is this?"

"Deal works for me, Mae."

"The hell you say." She held out her hand, which Deal shook, and he found it was just a shade smaller than his and firm. Though her eyes brushed over the burn mark on his face, it was more an approving caress. "Deal? . . . yup, Deal Calloway. Mort Elkol spoke highly of you. Well, my place is packed, and what the hell are you gents gonna have?" She threw that over her shoulder, and this to a waitress, "Tillie, get your arse over to Jimbo's table pronto." And to the cook as she went behind the counter hedging next to the back kitchen, "Where the hell's that order for the Ridgway table; get the lead out, Soapy."

"Would you believe that long, long ago Mae was hitched to a sky pilot?"

73

Deal grinned, shot a glance at Jimbo Rood, and said to Lon, "I'd believe anything you tell me about her."

"Well she was. As I gather it lasted less'n six months. Lived down at Lander at the time. The years have been what she's made them for herself, some good, some bad, along with going through three or four husbands. Wouldn't surprise me none one day she pulls out of here to try somethin' else."

The interlude of eating at Mustang Mae's had instilled in Deal a sense of well-being. The center of attention had been Mae. He didn't have to spend the whole time thinking that everyone in the place was aware of his disfigurement. He expected that if he got into town more, after a while nobody would notice anything. Just like Mae, he should let it all hang out and be damned to what anybody thought. Jimbo Rood was still hanging on with them, as they barhopped around in a town where the saloons weren't crowded together but spread out. A lot of cowhands looking to hook on someplace had drifted in. Most of them were broke, but a few like Deal Calloway had wintered up at some line shack, and they were spending freely. Back when he'd left Colorado he'd been broke and sourly hurting, but since then Deal had salted away most of his wages. Tonight he'd bought his share of drinks, though.

The truth was, as Deal had to admit to himself, that he was enjoying this night on the town, even though it was Rood and Holter doing most of the talking. They accepted him; something he didn't want to shy away from. One of their stops had been in the Tyler Saloon, where a couple of waddies had begun hammering away at one another. So they'd left, to find a final saloon before Lon Holter called it a night.

One thing unusual about Frank Hutto was his ability to remember certain mannerisms of people he'd encountered years ago. He had left the others back at the hotel—there were times when he didn't like sharing a bottle. The truth was he just couldn't stand being around Pike Gear in the shape Gear was.

"Worse than some woman givin' birth to twins."

The fact Old Thermopolis was doing a thriving business this evening didn't help Hutto's mood either. There were a lot of cowboys and ranchers out taking advantage of the weather and the saloons. Maybe some lawmen sprinkled in there too, and this worried Hutto. He'd vacated one saloon when it got too crowded, and finding another, it was from a solitary back table that he took in the three cattlemen stirring the batwings to ease up to the bar. There was something about the bigger one, the one with the scarred face, those deliberate movements of his when he reached to pick up his shot glass, the wary eyes under the worn hat. Mused Frank Hutto at the time, *got that one earmarked as a lawman.* Even though Hutto had packed away about a half bottle of whiskey, it was there, something jogging his thoughts along his outlaw backtrail.

He got as far back as the San Luis Valley in southern Colorado when he knew, only to have the three men at the bar head outside. A wolfine grin creasing his shaggy-bearded face, Hutto muttered, "It was the one that got away; what the hell's his name? When we torched that U.S. marshal."

He left the bottle there in his eagerness to find out where the three who'd just left were heading. A name was beginning to nudge into the forefront of his mind. Out on the boardwalk, he could see people moving about to either side and across the street, but then it didn't matter, as he exclaimed, "Calloway, dammit! It was Deal Calloway! There's still a price on his head."

Collecting his thoughts, Frank Hutto knew that it wouldn't be all that hard tracking down a man who was branded the way Calloway was. Probably working at some ranch hereabouts. The man was a turncoat, the worst kind in the eyes of Frank Hutto. Those Englishmen had high hopes for the Big Horn Basin, and this Calloway was the one man who could see them fail. Turning to go upstreet, Hutto was of the mind he didn't want to tackle this hombre alone. As he recollected, Deal Calloway had a hairtrigger temper, used to be as mean as Pike Gear. And he wouldn't mind splitting that bounty money with Gear and Kling and Slater Green; they'd be making a lot more soon's Jock La Prele reached Old Thermopolis.

When Hutto had trudged back to the Archer Hotel, he found Pike Gear easing out of a big galvanized copper bathtub, and Gear saying from here he meant to hit the sack. "So, Frank, I'll see you in the morning."

"I don't wanna tackle him alone."

"Who, some drunken swamper?" jeered Gear as he draped a second towel around his bare shoulders.

"You'll change your tune, Pike, when I tell you its him, Calloway. We've struck ourselves a windfall, Pike. Saw him just a little bit ago, downstreet at some bar. Him and two others."

"Hand me that bottle," muttered Pike Gear. He knew

that when carrying a load Hutto could generally be expected to see a lot of things, a lot of them imagined. He gurgled down some whiskey, and lowering the bottle, stared at Hutto through skeptical eyes.

"Pike, his face is all chewed up from what that hot tar did to it. But I know it's Calloway; we rode with him for what, goin' on a year. Them Englishmen . . ."

"Dammit, Frank, I told you about keepin' your flap shut about the Claretons. From what La Prele told me, they've changed their names. This is my last warnin' about that, you hear?"

"You know me when I get liquored up," he said nervously. "Five thousand is the price on Deal Calloway's head."

"Okay, Frank, lighten up. Say it is Calloway you seen tonight. The last thing La Prele warned us about was startin' a ruckus up here."

"You mean just up and forget that bounty money?"

"Nope, we ain't forgettin' no windfall. Just that we'll take him from ambush."

"Tonight you mean?"

"He's here ain't he? What better time than tonight? Crowded as this cow town is, there's no way the local law can pin the blame on us. Tomorrow if La Prele shows up we'll take credit for the killing. Now go find Soddy and Slater Green. Then we'll go barhopping."

A suggestion from Jimbo Rood brought them out of the Red River Bar and toward Chubby Dexter's cafe, located at the other end of the short street and by the horses tied outside still doing a late-night business. If anything, it was warmer than it had been at sundown, the street where they were walking soggy under their boots. Off to their right a honky-tonk was drawing some cowhands in to see the girls, and Rood said idly, "When I was younger I supported places like that."

"You ever think of gettin' married, Jimbo?" inquired Lon Holter.

"About all I've ever gotten is to the thinkin' stage," he said. "What about you, Deal?"

Out from the saloon they'd just vacated strode a couple of ranchers, and one of them called out, "Hey, Lon, hold up. I need to talk to you."

Pausing with the others, Deal Calloway in turning let the bullet slap past that was meant to tear into his chest. Instead the slug from the gun of Pike Gear struck into Lon Holter. From Holter came a gasp of shock and pain, and he tumbled down. Jimbo Rood clawed for his holstered gun even as Deal Calloway's gun answered the muzzle flashes of that first gun and others being fired by the ambushers.

Deal heard a yelp of pain just before the shooting cut away, and he broke that way, coming in on the deeper shadows alongside a frame building. A gun belched flame at him, an ambusher, the one who'd been hit, reeling out into the street. He sustained two quick slugs from Deal's sixgun, and the man went down hard, face first into a puddle of water. Now when Deal got in by the side wall, he could make out the dim forms of the rest of them coming in under some trees and brush closer to the river. His finger triggered the gun, but the hammer thudded onto an empty chamber. He started that way, reloading as he went, then it came to him that Lon Holter had been hit.

"Sonsofbitches," he barked after them as he came to

an abrupt halt in a wide empty lot. He trotted back still gripping his sixgun, one angry eye for the body of the dead ambusher, but his concern now was for the man he worked for lying in the middle of the street.

Deal came in closer, where Jimbo Rood looked up at Deal where he was squatting down as another rancher was trying to stem the flow of blood coming from an ugly wound just under Holter's armpit.

The rancher said, "That slug angled in close to the heart," to which Jimbo Rood threw in, "They've sent for a doctor. Deal, we'll carry Lon over to Chubby's place."

Carefully five of them lifted Lon Holter up to bring him in the back door of the cafe, with Deal one of them and cradling an arm under Holter's shoulders. Hurriedly another table was brought back into the kitchen, and with two of them pushed together, they lowered the rancher down, where he groaned and blinked his eyes open.

He had a wan smile for the faces spread out above him, and somehow he got out, "Saturday nights can . . . get rowdy . . . Deal, I . . ."

"They sent for a doctor, Lon," Calloway said softly.

"There was . . . there was more than one gun?"

Jimbo Rood nodded, and he said, "At least four of them. Maybe they mistook us for some others. As I don't make any sense out of this."

"Okay," Chubby Dexter said curtly, "here's Doc Youmans. Coffee and any grub you want is on me, so ease up front, boys. Yup, Doc, been heatin' water . . ."

How could Deal Calloway, as he slipped out the back door as did some others, respond to the questions just asked in there by Jimbo Rood? Should he just come out

79

and tell it as he believed it, that the bullet which cut down Lon Holter was meant for him? This act of violence a matter of days after he'd cut down that man on up at the line shack, another man out of his past. That Bat Ridley had been up on Washakie Needles was just a quirk of fate. But he'd come purposely into the Big Horn Basin; of this Deal had no doubts.

He found himself strolling over to men clustered about the dead ambusher lying in the muddy street. When he got in closer, Deal looked at the town marshal, who was holding a lantern and said to Deal, "I hear you took this one out."

"Yup," he said somberly, and as he gazed down at the dead man. The body had been turned onto its back, and the man's shirt used to wipe the mud away to reveal a cruel, bearded face grimacing in death. Deal stood there, trying to probe just how it had been back in Colorado.

The trouble was a whole heap of them drifted in to be a part of the Clareton brothers crooked empire. Some didn't stick around long, and a lot got killed. Right now he could say he recognized this ambusher, but it would be a lie. And right now there was a chore that needed doing.

He threw out a glance that took in everyone there, and Deal Calloway said, "I've got a chore to do right now."

He turned and headed for Main Street, not telling them he must carry news of what happened to her husband to Marge Holter. When he kept on heading to the west after crossing the street, those still sighting in on Deal knew where he was going.

As for Deal Calloway, as he faded into the night on

a narrow lane that brought him ever closer to some houses cloaked in darkness, he knew that everything had changed. No longer could he leave the basin. His past was here, maybe as bloody and as violent as before. He would take a stand, not only because another man had taken a bullet meant for him, but because Deal knew the time for running was over.

"Yup, the basin is as good a place as any to die."

Six

Along with being the stock handler at the Birdseye stage station, Otto Kluger kept the station supplied with game birds or deer or elk. The refugee from Germany was a rifleman, having learned how to handle firearms after being conscripted into a Prussian infantry unit. But he left the art of the fast draw to hardeyed drifters passing through on their way to the Montana goldfields.

Most likely they'd stop at Charley's Spigot, a hog ranch sharing this lonely tract of windblown prairie. It didn't lie all that far from the stage station, less'n forty rods, and southerly, where lightning had charred a dying cottonwood.

At night Charley's would come alive. Cowhands would come in to check out the whores and to enjoy a sociable drink. Passengers overnighting at the stage station would meander over. But Otto Kluger had never set foot in the place, chiefly because he only knew a few words of this strange Western lingo. If he had a weakness, though, it was a craving for beer, and one memorable night this had got to him, as had the raucous music pushing in where he sat in the lee of the stage station. First he'd gone into the kitchen to get an empty bucket, and with this in hand had set out on foot on a worn path. Halfway there, it happened; gunfire erupted from the road ranch; then a man burst outside followed by several others. Kluger found out later it was a cheating card hustler. The man had broken Kluger's way in an attempt to reach the stage station. All Otto Kluger could think to do was to flop down and use the bucket as a shield against incoming bullets which were peppering around and into the luckless card hustler. Two bullets did penetrate the bucket, then the firing had stopped, and Kluger vowed at that moment to swear off drinking beer until he could find a more civilized place.

This morning Kluger had risen earlier than usual. He wanted to get into position down by the river before the deer would come down to drink. It had been a hard winter, and game animals would be thinned out. But even so, everyone at the stage station was getting tired of eating beefsteak. As usual, he'd gone on foot, tramping westerly a couple of miles, before daybreak and when it was windless and a mite chilly. A place he'd used before caught his eye, and he went there, across a gravelly stretch of bank to a sandbar angling out into the shallow waters of Wind River, and here he got in amongst brush and stunted trees.

He didn't have long to wait. Even before the sun had begun lidding over the horizon a small band of mule deer appeared. Removing a heavy work glove, he brought up the Henry, propping the barrel on a branch and ever so carefully worked the lever-trigger guard, the faint sound not picked up by the deer single-filing toward the river along an old game trail. They were north of him, where the river cut around a bend of high loamy soil etched with multi-colored layers.

Kluger decided to go for one of the bucks. At a distance of less than a hundred yards he knew it would only take one bullet to sever the backbone. On the deer came, angling down the long sloping bank covered with wispy white tendrils of dew, when all of a sudden they spooked, catching the scent of a wolf or coyote, some scattering away. The rifle bucked and the aim of the German went awry. The bullet struck the deer someplace in the chest, but it seemed to have no effect. The animal broke around the river bend, where it seemed to go to its knees, then sprang up again and disappeared.

Grimacing his displeasure, Kluger retraced his route off the sandbar and began the tedious and tiring process of tracking the wounded animal down.

"Not enough hunting this winter," he scolded himself, as his gait picked up along the riverbank. The sun was clearing now, and it threw his shadow out across the placid waters.

Without too much difficulty he made his way through brush and around the river bend, where fresh cloven hoofprints were embedded in the thawing mud bank. Then he stopped, uncertain of what he was seeing in flotsam pushed close to the river's edge. Under the bill of his black felt cap he set cautious eyes upon a dead tree branch and the object held in it. Going in closer, he realized to his dismay that it was a body.

Grasping an arm encased in a buckskin coat, he pulled the body in closer to the bank. The dead man lay belly down, and only when Kluger turned the body onto its side did a spasm of fear expel air from his lungs.

"This man ... he left with yesterday's stage for the basin."

Putting his rifle aside, he dragged the body out of the water, thinking, *It is the one they called Osage, the halfblood? What could have happened?* The clothing was wet and clung to the body, and with riverwater washing away any blood that could have seeped from the wounds that had killed Osage Mattson. This registered in Kluger's mind: outlaws had held up the stagecoach. And also that he must bring the body back to the stage station.

Otto Kluger was a big man, with wide shoulders and sturdy legs. He forgot the wounded deer now, and the wet clothing worn by the dead man, as he lifted the body up and placed it over a shoulder. Reaching for his rifle, he came up the riverbank and began beelining directly for the Birdseye stage station hidden behind a long ridgeline.

From the sanctuary of a porch fronting Charley's Spigot road ranch the watchful eyes of Jock La Prele had discerned the man on foot coming over a rise. At first it appeared the man was weighed down with a backpack, as it was still hazy out and La Prele had just woken up to come down from an upstairs bedroom. A cup of steaming hot coffee helped to chase away the aftereffect of last night's drinking.

He didn't say anything when Pony Bob Haslam came out on the front porch to claim part of the bench wedged in close to the log wall. Haslam had brought along a cup and a plate piled high with taters and beefsteak. Once a pony express rider, when that business had petered out, Pony Bob had tried muleskinnin' before hooking up with La Prele. Chomping away at a mouthful of taters, it took him a moment to follow La Prele's northerly gaze and notice the distant figure just touching onto the stagecoach road.

"Could be trouble."

He looked aslant at La Prele, and before responding, he washed the food down with some coffee. "How'd you figure, Jock? We just got here an'll leave peaceable as we came."

"We're a couple of days late, Pony Bob. Maybe that man he's packing in is alive, just got a broken leg or something. You hold in here while I amble over to the stage station." All he got as he rose was an indifferent nod from Haslam stabbing his fork into the taters.

Men such as Pony Bob and the ten others stirring into wakefulness inside the hog ranch never could read the danger signs. Unlike an alley cat gifted with nine lives, Pony Bob would use up less than a quarter of the only one he had before he got himself killed. The man was what, twenty-two, and had carved up and gunned down at least half a dozen. And so, steeped in the arrogance that his sixgun would bail him out of any scrape, he sat back on that shaded porch pigging down an early breakfast. While Jock La Prele, as he came in on the side wall of the stage station, was getting this inkling they should stay out of the Big Horn Basin.

His mood wasn't improved by the telegram he'd received from Thomas Clareton stating that the Englishman and his brother had encountered certain difficulties and they'd be delayed. "Doesn't matter all that much," La Prele muttered, "as the groundwork's been laid."

Though they'd been run out of Colorado, it hadn't bothered La Prele all that much. He considered his time

86

spent down there a learning experience. It all came down to something called equity. Not of money so much or property, but what La Prele figured was more in the form of equity of the mind. A man could go busted in a high stakes game, but if he understood how the game was played, next time he could come out a winner. Whether it was cards or dice or, as in this case, the land business. Right now the only reason he needed the Claretons was that these killing highbinders had a lot of greenbacks. In Colorado, mused Jock La Prele, despite everything he'd been just another hired gun. Up here it would be a helluva lot different. Now he'd be the one stacking the deck.

Coming around the corner of the stage station, with the corrals and two sheds, off to his left, and an open-sided blacksmith shop, he drew up short. Three men, the one with the string tie and the longsleeved shirt he figured to be the station manager, were hurrying away from the buildings toward Otto Kluger, who was bending to lower the body down onto the road.

La Prele spat out chaw juice. A mule, one of a pair in one of the corrals, brayed as it caught the scent of death. The voice of the German came gibberishly to the gunfighter. He could make out a name, which carried little meaning, but the reactions of the others explained it all to La Prele. Now the voice of the station manager came back plain. "They must have hit the stage this side of the mountains."

What could these men do, La Prele wondered? The closest lawman was at least fifty miles away. He could have drawn back around the main building and made tracks back to the hog ranch. But, craftily, Jock La Prele knew he could use this to his advantage. He went on toward where they were picking up the dead body of Osage Mattson. His glance picked out station manager Russ Dixon. "I couldn't help overhearing what happened."

"Mister," Dixon said curtly, "we don't know what happened yet. All we know is that Mattson left on yesterday's coach. You're not from around here?" Suspicion framed Russ Dixon's deepset eyes. He was stocky and not all that tall, but had about him a look of reliability.

La Prele jabbed a thumb southerly. "Me and some other waddies are headin' up into the basin. We're hopin' to hook on for the summer at some spread."

"That so?"

"Look," shrugged La Prele, "I'm offerin' to help. Seems to me right now you need a lot of that."

"Sorry," Dixon said, as he let the others carry the body inside the stage station. "I run this place. I'm Russ Dixon."

"Sam Morgan, out of Utah, around Provo."

"How many men do you have?"

"Less'n a dozen, Mr. Dixon. Cowpokes like me. I gather that stage was bound for the basin."

"Yup, and it left yesterday. Haven't had this kind of trouble in a long time, Mr. Morgan. The German, Kluger, found the halfblood's body in the river. River's two, three miles west of the main road?"

"If the stage was held up," speculated La Prele, "there could have been gunplay. Or afterwards the stage kept on into the basin."

"Since you're heading up that way, Mr. Morgan, I'd appreciate any help you could give us."

"Sure, I'll head back to that road house and roust out

the others." He turned as Dixon went into the stage station, and Jock La Prele picked up his pace a little. Anger was stirring in La Prele; trouble of this kind could work against them. Once the stage line got word about what had happened to Cheyenne, some U.S. marshals were sure to show up. What happened down in Colorado, those two lawmen going down under the guns of his men, along with that U.S. marshal they'd set fire to after he'd been bathed in hot tar, could bring federal lawmen into the Big Horn Basin. The latest report La Prele had received from some of the land agents the Claretons had sent up there spoke of the basin being a backward and isolated place.

Jock La Prele wasn't in the best frame of mind when he closed in on the hog ranch, where three more hardcases besides Pony Bob were taking their ease. His eyes singled out Gus Devol as he said flatly to everyone, "Soon's you finish chowin' down we're moving out. Pony Bob, saddle my horse." He opened the screen door to enter, followed by Devol. The pair of them claimed a table.

"Was he dead?"

"One of the men working at the stage station packed the body in from the river."

"Maybe this hombre drowned."

"No such luck. He left on yesterday's stage for Old Thermopolis." La Prele fell silent as one of the whores doing double duty as a waitress deposited a bottle of whiskey and two glasses on the table. He ignored the woman as he studied his table companion, and then with an indifferent shrug she returned to the bar. He knew he could trust dour and horsey-faced Gus Devol. The man was more gambler than hardcase or gunhand.

Before, when they'd been in Colorado, Devol was generally clad in trousers and a black coat and string tie. But not at the moment. La Prele had given orders that everyone was to wear the workaday garb of a cowpuncher. "You miss Reno?" He gurgled whiskey into the glasses.

"Stayin' in one place suited me, Jock. Just got unlucky at cards one night." He flashed a wry smile, then sipped from the glass. He flexed the fingers of his left hand. "Rheumatic fever, they call it. But I still can hold my own in most cow towns. So, I'm listening."

"We're gonna ride along with the manager of the stage station. Uptrail, I expect, until we come across something. You'll have to stay here in my place, Gus. Look for the Claretons to show up any day, an' don't leave until they do."

"Sure, Jock. They could ask why you're not here."

Emptying his glass, La Prele came to his feet. From his wallet he removed some greenbacks, which he laid on the table top. "Thomas Clareton knows I'm the cautious type. This stagecoach incident, a damned fool stunt."

"Could be none of the men you hired were in on it, Jock. At least they were told to come in peaceable."

He speared Devol with a slitted eye. "Some of them haven't got the brains of a jackrabbit. But I reckon in this game we take what we can get."

"Obliged for the whiskey."

The farewell words of the other hardcase followed Jock La Prele out the door. Most of his men were over by the corral tending to their horses. When they saw La Prele, they mounted up and came toward him while he sidled a glance at a couple of others just exiting from the

90

back door of the hog ranch. Nodding as Pony Bob handed him the reins of his horse, a deep-bellied grey, La Prele eased into the saddle.

"Those stragglers can catch up," he said, and then he spurred toward the stage station.

The stage station manager went along with Jock La Prele's sage advice that they split into two bunches. So about half of them kept to the main road. La Prele had purposely gone west with the rest of them, including Russ Dixon, to ride in close along the river. A spring wind came yowling across the floodplain, bringing in tufts of clouds.

As he rode alongside Dixon, La Prele kept up a quiet flow of conversation. "I hear it doesn't get all that windy up in the basin."

"Sometimes a Chinook meanders in, Mr. La Prele. But generally there isn't enough wind to ruffle a woman's bonnet. Too bad that ranch of yours went belly-up."

"Just too many dry years. My wife took off, was in Oregon someplace last I heard. You said your family is on the way out from Chicago."

"The only thing that will be the same for them is the wind. Agnes, she's city born and reared; living at the stage station might be too much of a change."

"At least she agreed to give it a try, Mr. Dixon."

Up ahead of them, Otto Kluger and four men working for La Prele passed around the river bend where Kluger had wounded that mule deer. Just behind them rode a stock handler holding onto the halter ropes of a pair of horses wearing harnesses, with a pack on one horse holding some shovels. Russ Dixon hoped they wouldn't have to use the shovels; he hoped that the stagecoach had in fact gone on to Old Thermopolis. Rarely had the tedium of daily life been shattered by a holdup in the two years Dixon had come out to take charge at Birdseye.

This time of year it wasn't as hazy as it would be in midsummer, when it got a lot warmer, and they could see into the southern approaches to the Wind River Canyon. The walls of the canyon were part of different mountain chains. And then the brush would choke up more, and the scrub trees, and they would lower their glances in sweeping circles along the wide pebbly bank of the river. They were about three miles out now, and La Prele made the remark that the men keeping to the road would be making better time.

"Yup," said Dixon, "once the road clears Muddy Creek it bends easterly around the Bridgers. I'm hoping they don't pick up the tracks of the coach leaving the road."

At the distant barking of a handgun some birds wheeled out of the screening brush. Then two more shots were heard, and La Prele said, "They've found something."

Ahead of them, Kluger gestured at some turkey vultures rising up from the floodplain, whereupon Pony Bob Haslam shouted back, "Look at them damned vultures flushing up."

Tugging his hat down from the rising wind, Dixon jabbed a spur to send his horse into a canter. Then everyone was reining on harder, with yet another slight curl in the river and the brush hiding the dread of their expectancy. Anxiously they took in the upper part of the stagecoach coming into view from over the screening bank, and just that quickly they were in clear view of vultures winging away in protest from the scattering of what remained of the passengers and driver and shotgun. Their horses refused to go any further, and they began swinging down, grimacing as they did from the stench of rotting flesh.

"At least," Jock La Prele threw out, "they were dead before the birds got to them. What manner of men would do something like this?"

Grimly Russ Dixon said, "All we can do now is see they're buried proper. Mr. La Prele, we can tend to that. I know you want to get up into the basin."

"Nope, we'll stay and lend a hand. I expect you'll want me to report this to the sheriff up at Old Thermopolis."

"Yes, these men must be caught and punished."

Moving in closer, as did Dixon, La Prele said, "That must be the banker you told me about."

"Yes, Mr. Blaine. He was such a nice gentleman. Told me, that night at the stage station, about coming up to see his wife."

"Blaine—knew some from Oklahoma."

"As a matter of fact Mr. Blaine was from Oklahoma City. Now, we might as well put those shovels to use."

Jock La Prele let it go at that, flicking his eyes to the other bunch coming their way from the east over higher ground. He knew all about how Justin Blaine had been bankrolling his wife in her search for the killers of her brother. He'd pieced this together during the past year, but until now had figured the woman more of a nuisance than a serious threat to their present setup. If she was in the basin, this Cleo Blaine, there'd also be her brother and a few others.

The idea came to Jock La Prele when he was coming onto the stagecoach road again. They'd stuck around long enough to help bury the dead, and now, he realized it would be just him bringing word up into the basin about the killings. Since no telegraph line ran into the basin. Those who'd held up the stagecoach had left behind a scattering of letters and newspapers, which La Prele had in a leather pouch tied to his saddle along with a letter that Russ Dixon wanted him to deliver to the Big Horn County sheriff, and which he was about to tear into yellow shreds.

Once he reached Old Thermopolis, he'd composed another letter detailing how some outlaws led by a bandito named Cleo Blaine had held up the stage. Let Johnny Law take care of her, he mused around the lifting scent of a Mex cigarette. But he still intended to find out who the real highwaymen were, and if they chanced to be some of his rawhiders, they'd have to face his guns. For by holding up that stage they'd challenged his leadership.

"I'll find out," he muttered to the wind that was whipping southeasterly small scraps of yellowed paper.

Seven

Park County rancher Lon Holter didn't know of the birth of another granddaughter the day after he'd been gravely wounded. He lay in a coma in the southwest bedroom, unaware of the doctor's prognosis that he might never fully recover, or of the presence of Marge Holter. She sat gazing at her husband's hands folded over the coverlet. Lon's hands were a history of what it meant to hack out a living in the basin. They had been cut by rope and barbed wire, knew the touch of a gun and the licking tongue of a newborn calf, knew the feel of her body. They were large and still looked in control of all that Lon Holter was. But her husband's face told Marge Holter just how it was, the color drained away and the labored air coming out of his mouth as he fought to stay alive.

Though the windows were ajar, no wind stirred the flowery blue drapes that had been pulled aside to let in late afternoon sunlight. She was tired, and ought to be, for Marge Holter had never left her husband's side, except for the brief moments she'd stretched out on a small cot her daughter's husband and Deal Calloway had carried in here. Patiently she reached toward the small basin on the bedstand and dipped the towel into cold water. After rinsing the towel out, she folded it neatly and placed it on Lon's forehead. He never stirred, and the raspy sound of his breathing brought worry to her eyes. She trailed her fingers alongside his cheek caressingly, then pushed wearily to her feet, for there was a chore that must be tended to, one that involved Deal Calloway.

From a dresser she picked up a dark blue shawl, which she arranged around her shoulders. In her was a chill, a dread that Lon might not pull out of this. As she came out of the bedroom, she looked at her son-in-law framed in the doorway of the bedroom occupied by the new mother and baby. "At least they are healthy," Marge Holter said gratefully, upon entering the kitchen, where a savory aroma wafted away from a kettle heating on the iron range. In the sink were some dishes that needed washing and a second-hand clock ticked away on one of the shelves in the cabinet Lon had made last winter. Just for a moment she could picture his hands using a plane to smooth the wood; the wistful moment passed as she found the back screen door.

Some ranchers were still out back, as was Pitchfork segundo Jimbo Rood and Deal Calloway. Her presence on the burned-out expanse of back lawn brought them to their feet from where'd they been seated around a picnic table placed under a large oak tree. Come summer that tree cast down cooling shade, and Marge Holter remembered the time—no, mustn't go chasing up how it had been, too painful now.

"Missus Holter," a man said awkwardly, and she vaguely recollected him as a rancher from away north in

Park County. "I can tell you don't remember me, but I'm Walt Thiel. Your husband bought some cattle from me, couple years back."

"Of course, Walt, I do remember," she smiled. "How sweet of you to come by. I do hope all of you boys will stay on for supper."

"Well, I," said another rancher.

"But I insist," she said, "won't be any bother at all."

"Why sure, Marge," said moon-faced George Mahan under the drooping handlebar mustache, as he'd known her longer than anyone here. Around seventy, Mahan had leased out his land to another rancher, and sometimes in the spring he would be at this ranch or another helping out with calfing. That she just wanted company and to busy herself with throwing together a meal to take her thoughts off of Lon was plain as the smile still holding to her face. She'd been there when his Anne had passed away, and he added jestingly, "Now, Marge, don't throw on nothin' fancy . . . say some steak and frys and . . ."

"And," she threw back, "some apple pie. What you can do, Mr. Mahan, is help us decorate this picnic table with eatin' hardware. Deal, could we talk—"

When Marge and Deal Calloway pushed on past the oak tree to the lee of a shed, the others settled down again. Deal was apprehensive, and he felt guilty because his presence here in Old Thermopolis had brought harm to Lon Holter. He was hatless, with his sleeves rolled halfway up his muscular forearms, watching as she went on a couple of feet to an apple tree growing next to the shed.

Marge Holter brought a finger touching onto a scaly fissure in an upthrusting branch, and she said, "Too early for it to bud; but this weather keeps up." She stood there as he came in closer, then to Deal's surprise she reached up and touched the burn mark on his face, then she withdrew her hand. "To me that burn mark is a badge of honor, not something to be ashamed of. Someday you'll meet another woman who'll tell you the same thing, Mr. Calloway. What I'm saying, Deal, is that you're about the best waddy we've ever had."

"Why, ma'am, I'm obliged for that."

"You did promise Lon you'd hold on until after calfing was over. But I know Lon wouldn't hold you to that now, Deal. As I know those bullets were meant for you."

"Cut and run," he said acridly. "I do that now, I'd be running all my life. Lonetree—it's gotten to be a good place to hang my hat. I leave, I'd sure miss your cooking. I'll hang on, and I expect you'll put Mort Elkol in charge."

"Deal, I'd rather you handled operations at the ranch."

"I don't know."

"I can see it in you, that you love ranchin', and you sure can handle any chore that comes up. You see, it'll be a spell before Lon recovers. When he does, well, we've talked of selling Lonetree. I know you've been saving up; and Lon and I sure hope you'd consider buyin' us out."

"Why, Marge, I, I'd have to come up with a heap more than I've saved. Lonetree's, well, it would bring a high price on the open market."

"I expect so, Mr. Calloway. Money isn't everything. What counts is the friendship of men like you, and their loyalty."

"Now, it could be that Lon just might decide to hang in out there—"

"Leave that to me. I'll write you up an open letter of credit. Good in any town in the basin. Now don't fret about Lon—he'll recover.

"I reckon I shouldn't hang around too long. Maybe leave tomorrow, or day after. The wagon, I'll take that and load up with supplies.

"There is one favor I'll be asking, Deal. Tulips are early bloomers. Could you water them, and the other flowers when they began sprouting." She brought an embracing arm around his shoulder and gave him a hug.

And Deal said, "Marge, you're one in a million."

Through misting eyes she said, "You're a thoroughbred, Deal Calloway, saw that first day I laid eyes on you. And don't you be bashful about stagecoachin' a letter down to us about how you're doing. Now I'd best skedaddle into the kitchen and prepare you hungry galoots some grub."

He had been talked into one last night on the town by Jimbo Rood. He appreciated it, Rood's show of friendship. The fact that Lonetree was considerably smaller than the spread Rood worked for didn't seem to make any difference. They hadn't barhopped but stuck to one of Old Thermopolis's more sedate saloons, the Hole-In-The-Wall, which was famous throughout the territory for its cherry-wood bar.

The county meeting had broken up around midday, and out to their ranches went the cattlemen and a lot of waddies they'd taken on for the summer. Deal knew more cowhands would come stagecoaching in as spring really took hold or come in forking their own horses. Inevitably they would make this cow town their first stop, old hands who'd come back for years, and strangers. It was because of the latter element that Deal avoided cow towns this time of year.

He kept thinking about Lon Holter through the bantering talk he had going with Rood. During the day Big Horn County Sheriff Rollie Herslip had stopped by the house to get a statement from Deal and from Rood, and from anyone who might have witnessed the shooting. Herslip related that he hadn't found any identification on the dead ambusher, nor it seemed had anyone else gotten a glimpse of the others.

When the sheriff had begun to ask him some hard questions, Deal had been thankful for Marge Holter stepping in to defend him. What he'd told the Holters as to his past on the way in here was still fresh in her mind. He hadn't told all of it, but he'd made it clear that he'd ridden the lawbreaking trail. There she'd been, with the doctor still at her husband's bedside, coming back just as snappy at the sheriff. Now, knowing what he'd been, she had just entrusted him with running a place it had taken the Holters most of their lives to build into something.

Jimbo Rood waved back at some cattlemen he knew occupying a table, and he said to Deal, "Want to join them?"

"Going on eleven by that wall clock. I was meaning to tell you that Marge asked me to run Lonetree until Lon gets back on his feet."

"One thing about Marge, she's a keen judge of character. You'll handle it, Deal." Rood looked down the crowded bar for a bartender, then he crooked a beckoning finger that said fill their shot glasses up again. "This means, Deal, you'll be representing Lonetree at that meeting over at Meeteetse."

"In all that's happened I forgot about that."

"Ain't you that Lonetree hand, Calloway—"

Both of them half-turned from the bar to eye in on a cowhand gripping a bottle of corn whiskey. There'd been a whiskey slur to his voice, and Deal was quick to notice that he held the bottle with his off-hand.

"Yup," he smirked out, "you're him—ugly scar and all."

"What the hell you want?" Rood shot out.

"Ain't you heard? This big hunk of ugly here gunned down an outlaw away up on Washakie Needles." He swung around in a half-circle as silence descended on the saloon. He wasn't all that big, but from the set to his high-cheeked face the sixgun he packed made him just as big if not bigger than everyone in the place. "Yup, emptied the loads from that sixgun he's totin' before this outlaw could even get off one shot. Calloway—you must be good."

"Leave it be," Rood said as he shouldered in close to the drunken hand. "Get the hell out of here."

"Nobody lays a hand on me," the man flared back. "You, Calloway, are you really that good?"

Deal managed to control his anger as he stepped away from the bar with the intentions of leaving, only to have the cowhand nudge the bottle he carried at Deal's elbow. "Nobody walks out on me, Calloway. I heard that outlaw skinned Cal Egan while he was still alive. I heard he was fast, this Bat Ridley."

The fist launched by Deal had the full weight of his shoulder behind it, catching the cowhand flush in the nose. The force of it broke cartilage and splayed out blood, slamming the cowhand against the bar. He didn't move once he slid down to the floor. But Calloway did, shoving out through the batwings.

He pulled out in the morning, his saddle horse tied to the wagon, a man filled with uncertainties over whether he could handle the job of ramrodding Lonetree. One thing he was sure of was that this would be a summer of violence in the Big Horn Basin. They were coming in, maybe not the same crew, but if the Clareton brothers were moving in, they'd have on their payroll the gunfighters Jock La Prele and Pike Gear, and others that he'd ridden with.

"Me ownin' Lon Holter's Lonetree? Doesn't hardly seem possible."

Eight

Jock La Prele had sent his men on ahead, singly and in pairs, into Old Thermopolis. This was a lesson gleaned from the killing fields down in southern Colorado. He sent patient eyes westerly to the afterglow of sunset filtering through a jagged mass of mountains. According to a surveyor's map they were the Absarokas. He'd hate to cross them in any kind of weather.

He was letting his horse jog on the stagecoach road breaking out of the northern foothills of the Bridgers. He wasn't all that far out; there was still enough sunlight left for him to see river waters glinting dully and the buildings hugging the western bank of the Big Horn. Dark red hillocks humped up around the town.

Once he crossed the log bridge south of town, the gelding broke into a faster gait, and though La Prele was just as anxious to come to trail's end, he reined back to a jog. A man coming into a town at more'n a jog usually attracted some attention.

He came along Main Street. Up ahead lay the Chandler Hotel, but he bypassed it, veering toward the boardwalk to ask a passing townsman where the sheriff's office was located. Armed with the information, he kept along the street until it curved northeasterly, the courthouse off to his right, with no lights showing in the high stone building, at least until he got past the wide portico. There was a lower front door opening into the sheriff's office. Then someone came out, and La Prele said, "Sheriff Herslip?"

"Rollie's inside," the deputy said as Jock La Prele swung down. Figuring the stranger as just another cowhand, the deputy moved away.

Untying the leather pouch from his saddle, La Prele turned to stare at the gilded lettering on the pair of windows. Big Horn County Sheriff's Office. When he went inside, the front office was empty, which gave him an opportunity to study the wanteds pinned around the walls. He saw a few familiar faces; fortunately his wasn't one of them. The murmur of voices from the basement cellblock told him some prisoners were down there.

"Okay, Clancy, I'm calling it a day," came the voice of Sheriff Rollie Herslip as he tramped up the stone steps to the jingling of spurs. When he passed through the open door, he frowned at the man standing facing out a window.

Turning, La Prele said pleasantly, "Russ Dixon asked me to deliver this." He came forward and set the pouch on the desk behind which the sheriff had stepped. "Sorry to say, Sheriff, but the stage was held up."

"Do I know you?"

"Never been up here before. I drifted in out of Utah. In search of a ridin' job. I'm Sam Morgan. An', Sheriff Herslip, this letter Dixon gave me is for you." He handed it to Herslip, then he removed his hat and brushed a hand across his upper forehead, sighing

104

deeply before he added, "Everyone on the stage was killed."

Sheriff Herslip stopped reading, gazed at La Prele for a moment as if he didn't believe what he'd just heard. He was stolid, with a big head sunk into wide shoulders, his eyes registering pain as he said, "Everyone ... dead. It proved out to be the last ride for Dutch Trajon after all. This letter Dixon sent, says here some woman named Blaine is behind this, her and some others. If everyone was killed—"

"I was at the stage station when this man came stumbling in. Came in from the river instead of the main road, a cowpoke, Osage Mattson. He'd left with the stage. Before he died he managed to get out what happened."

"I knew him, Osage."

"I went along to hunt for the stage; found it up by the river. At first these outlaws left a trail that was easy to follow—but it petered out in the Bridgers."

"Means they're either here in the basin. Or could be part of the Hole-In-The-Wall bunch, be heading for the Big Horns. Morgan, you look more like a cattleman than some cowpuncher."

"I was, once, a rancher. Lack of rainwater busted me and some others."

"The way of it in dry times."

"Didn't get much for my place. Maybe I can find a banker up here who'll grubstake me to another place."

"All the bankers I know throw nickels around like manhole covers."

"I know the kind, Sheriff. If you don't need a loan they're barkin' at your front door just to get a part of what you've got. So, some mail's in that pouch. I'm stayin' at the Chandler Hotel until I line up something."

"Obliged for this, Mr. Morgan."

After the stranger had left, Sheriff Rollie Herslip slumped down, the swivel chair creaking under him. He finished reading the letter, a one page recap of the stage holdup. This shooting the other night in which the only casualty had been a Park County rancher, was there a connection? Nope, he finally decided, the shooting happened about the same time. The county judge would have to be told about the holdup, and he would have to get word up into the basin to Elmo Cowley and other lawmen. One thing that worked in favor of lawbreakers up here was the lack of any railroad or telegraph lines connecting the spread of cow towns—though the *Basin Gazette* printed here in Old Thermopolis had carried a story in one of last month's issues that some company had plans to string telegraph wire up along the Big Horn River to Worland and Greybull.

He rose and put the letter into a coat pocket as he leaned over the desk to blow out the lamp. By the door, he took his low-crowned hat from a wall peg and went outside. It still hadn't settled in that Dutch Trajon was dead, along with some others. He didn't want to believe the contents of the letter, but Sam Morgan had verified that. Any thoughts of having supper were forgotten as Sheriff Rollie Herslip crossed the street and went down a lane that would take him to Judge Cedric Barlow's gabled house, the first building a person would sight in on when coming in from the north.

"Sure was looking forward to spring. Now these killings have happened."

Once the word was spread around that Jock La Prele was in town, a land agent by the name of Bracy Hume showed up at the Chandler Hotel. He was dandied up in a dark brown twilled broadcloth suit. Up here he was using his real name. No one would remember a defrocked minister from North Carolina, while the gambling fraternity of the West knew him as the Euchre Kid. He'd brought along a plain black valise. Entering the dining room, he smiled toothily at La Prele sipping coffee laced with brandy. He sat down at the table. The other occupants of the high-ceilinged room were some waitresses preparing tables for the noon rush and one old-timer staring vacantly at a painting that depicted cattle stampeding in a lightning storm and a cowhand astride a horse casting back a wild cerulean eye to show its fear of the moment. As the old-timer pushed to his feet he passed gas, loudly, then he tottered out.

"At least there's someone," La Prele said sarcastically, "knows what he's doing. What have you got?" He turned an empty cup over and filled it with coffee from a ceramic server.

"Though we've managed to buy up some land, what you've got up here in the basin is a tight-knit bunch." Hume had a melodious Southern drawl which became filled with a lot of expletives when he got excited. Dropping a couple of cubes of sugar into his cup, he reached down and lifted out of the valise a plat map of the Big Horn Basin. He'd opened a temporary office a block from the county courthouse, and sometimes he would bring potential customers in here. He explained this after La Prele threw a wary glance around the dining room.

When he spoke again, he very carefully used the name La Prele had registered under. "So, Mr. Morgan, I've outlined in red the sections of land we've been able to purchase."

"Not all that much," retorted La Prele.

"But land that is connected to waterways; the kind of property that doesn't come cheap. Here, here, and here, these ranches aren't all that far from Old Thermopolis. So far we've been gently persuasive"—he brought a spoon chinking about in his cup—"but these folks won't sell out."

"That'll change once the Claretons pull in. Right now, Euchre, I'm more interested in how the law operates around here."

"So far no U.S. marshals have been assigned to work out of the basin; they come in on occasion, leave."

"This might change because of those stagecoach killings. Slaughtered all of them, and why?"

"They were probably from the basin, knew somebody on that stage . . ."

"Yeah, probably." La Prele let it go at that, as he refilled his cup, but didn't pour in any brandy from his flask this time.

"Pike Gear stopped by to see me."

"Gear? When did he pull in?"

"Couple of days ago, I expect. Sure, it was the day after that shooting here in town."

"Meaning that Pike could'a been in town before he came to see you, a couple of days or more. Tell me about it, that shooting."

"Some rancher was shot coming out of some saloon,

so the story goes. You know, come to think on it, Pike did throw some name at me. Then he sort of shut up about it." He could see La Prele's eyes getting flintier. Both of them had been involved with Pike Gear down in Colorado. They knew that Gear could be docile for days at a time, then something would set him off and he'd go off and pull a job someplace.

"Okay, Euchre, Pike was in to see you. Did he say anything about holding up a stagecoach?"

"You know how he is when he's drinking. But when he came in he was damned sober. Said something about collecting some bounty money—on a man named Calloway."

"So this is where he went." The irritance in La Prele's eyes changed to a pondering glaze. A man marked as Deal Calloway was shouldn't have been all that hard to find. They'd lost him that night, and somehow he ex- pected that Calloway had died. Now Pike Gear had stumbled upon Calloway. It would be like Pike to hit from ambush. "But to do it right here in town," he said lowly, angrily. "You happen to know where Gear is stay- ing?"

"I took a lease on the old Baker place—upriver about three miles. Pike said he'd head up there. Told Pony Bob about it too, Jock. You're saying that Pike shot that rancher?"

"Damn fool could ruin everything," snapped La Prele.

"I saw the headlines in the *Basin Gazette* about that stagecoach robbery. But that couldn't have been any of your men, Jock. They know better, or at least they should."

"Funny how the past has a way of coming in to haunt

109

you. I doubt any of those you spoke words over at some funeral will ever come back from the dead, Euchre."

Solemnly and through a toothy smile Bracy Hume intoned, "Only when the Rapture comes and the Lord returns to raise the living and the dead. Fleeced them good, the sheep that used to flock in to hear me preach. Until one day they caught me, me and this plantation owner's missus, both of us naked as jaybirds and humpin' away in one of the pews."

Despite the troubled frame of mind eating away at him, Jock La Prele forced a grin. He knew worry over things you couldn't control could destroy a man faster'n anything. After they'd been driven out of Colorado a few dry years had set in. La Prele had eked out a living as a small town marshal over in Oregon for one thing, and mostly kept to places he wasn't known.

At forty-seven he didn't have all that many good years left. But he was still faster at the draw than any man in his crew of outlaws, petty thieves and killers. They knew it, as did the Claretons. What he had in mind could bankroll him to something down in Argentina. There'd be no more cow town sheriffs eyeballing him, and he'd be rid of the likes of Pike Gear and Pony Bob, and those greedy Englishmen.

Three months ago La Prele had received a telegram to hook up with Thomas Clareton over at Salt Lake City. This was when he'd gotten word out that operations would be commencing with the arrival of spring in Wyoming. While there, it was revealed to Jock La Prele that the other Clareton brother, Francis, had been ailing; just consumption Thomas had led him to believe. It had taken a hundred dollars for the pious Mormon doctor to break his Hippocratic oath by revealing to La Prele that Francis Clareton had incurable cancer.

"Just a matter of time," he mused silently. They were a team, these Claretons. The quiet one, Francis, was the man La Prele made out to be the thinker and most persuasive when dealing with a banker, whereas handsome Thomas Clareton was the front man. It was the same in Salt Lake as it had been in Colorado; Thomas was unable to stay away from the women and the gambling. One thing about this younger brother, La Prele had learned, was that Thomas was always eager to strike any kind of deal providing he came out on top. But what Jock La Prele wanted, and was determined to get when the Claretons got up here, was an equal partnership.

"How many land buyers you got on the payroll, Euchre?"

"Three right now—more expected in."

"The county judge?"

"Cedric Barlow is kind of hard to deal with. One thing is he seems to be independently wealthy. And if you ain't from the basin you ain't nobody. Barlow's an' old clannish wardog; was in the Civil War, I picked up."

"I know the kind, Euchre. Like that statue out in front of the county courthouse—be there forever, unless . . ."

"Here, Jock, the towns are located along the rivers. I was up at Meeteetse. Sets right pretty in the Greybull Valley, and is centrally located. Be a nice place to set up headquarters."

"Up here yonder, Cody, the county seat of Park County. Look how isolated Cody is." He swept his hand over the plat map. "All we have to do is control one county seat."

111

"That's Buffalo Bill's stomping grounds."

Countered La Prele, "Cody's off someplace with that Wild West show of his. Big, this basin—but nothing we can't whittle down to size."

Nine

The caravan which crossed the river south of Old Thermopolis was made up of a Mormon wagon and two surreys. Gus Devol was one of a pair of outriders, but ever since leaving the Birdseye stage station he'd been riding in Thomas Clareton's carriage. The long day's ride to the first waystop in the basin, Old Thermopolis, had been tempered by a poker game. A table had been rigged up between the seats, and Devol had played alongside Matt Segelke, a land buyer out of Salt Lake City, who'd been between jobs when hiring on with Thomas Clareton's newly formed Continental Divide Land Company.

Another change taking place in Utah was that now the Claretons would be known as the Wolcott brothers. This was how the new advertising they had put out read. Devol didn't care what Thomas Clareton called himself as long as he got paid. Shuffling the deck, he had a smile for the woman pouring Devol corn whiskey into his glass. She had a cultured voice, though with just a trace of a Kansas-ricochet twang, and was possessed of silky auburn hair and sultry eyes. Her name was

Simone Jules, and she'd still be in Utah had not some Mormon elders closed the brothel she ran in Copper Creek. He figured her to be sharing Clareton's bed, and let it go at that as he dealt Simone Jules a card.

Side curtains had been added to the surrey, which were thonged up giving the passengers glances at the changing landscape in the basin. About a mile out of Old Thermopolis, the driver of the other surrey pulled off the road and reined up. The other vehicles trailed in behind, everyone getting out to stretch and get a better look at what lay ahead. Thomas Clareton moved up to the other surrey, which had its curtains down. Lifting a curtain aside, he leaned in and had a quick smile for the woman tending to his brother. The seats had been taken out back in Utah, a cot put in and a padded stool.

The eyes of Francis Clareton opened to protest the inflow of bright sunlight. He had lost even more weight since leaving Utah. A ghostly luminosity seemed to outline his bony face. He was bundled up in a heavy woolen robe over which lay two blankets. His hair lay in greying strands alongside his head, and the stench of medicine was strong in the cramped interior. He had accepted the fact that he was dying, and Francis Clareton smiled when the woman laid her hand over his.

"The curative springs at Old Thermopolis," she said, "should help you." Receiving a wan nod, she turned on the stool and held out her hand to Thomas Clareton as he helped her out of the surrey. Lydia Reinhold had been nursing Francis Clareton since midwinter, and she'd never expected to leave Salt Lake City. But she had because she'd fallen in love with the other brother, Thomas. She was an attractive brunette, full of body but not overly bold as was the other woman on this excursion into territorial Wyoming. Unlike Simone Jules, who was decked out rather extravagantly in an expensive satin dress and fur stole, Lydia Reinhold wore a plain gingham dress, and her hair was braided into one long strand hanging down her back.

His fingers tightened possessively on her hand as Thomas Clareton whispered, "You've been a godsend on this trip." He moved with her out of earshot of the surrey, to some naked chokeberry bushes encircled by other brush. Just beyond this was the west bank of the Big Horn River, whose waters were rising from the warmer weather bringing down snowmelt from the mountains. "I'm afraid it won't be much longer. We should have stayed there. But Francis insisted on coming along; a final voyage, he said."

"I'm about out of morphine."

"We'll replenish that and anything else Francis needs once we're settled into our hotel." He was a cigar smoker, but at the moment he refrained from lighting one up. There was a fear in him of what would happen when Francis was gone. Older by five years, Francis Clareton had always managed to keep them out of the clutches of the law. Their first big con game had involved the London Stock Exchange. The scheme was short-lived, but out of it they'd made enough money to sail for America. Entraining out of New York, they worked one con game after another, until in Chicago the wily Francis Clareton began selling shares in a cattle company which he claimed to own. Too late did those who'd purchased stock from the Claretons discover there weren't any cattle. From here the agile mind of Thomas's older brother brought them into Colorado.

115

Now here we are, Thomas Clareton mused worriedly, going into business again. In the past he'd simply let his brother handle any legal or business matters. Somehow he felt as if Francis was betraying him. He was tempted to pull out of here, but they'd already bought up ranch acreage. No, they'd invested too much money. And there were the reports he'd received from the land agents about the Big Horn Basin showing a lot of promise.

"Is there something wrong, Mr. Wolcott?"

"Ah, just that it's been a long trip," he replied. "We'd best be heading in."

They were alone, Thomas and his brother, Francis, and the malignant enemy spreading through Francis's ribcage. A local doctor had arrived to administer some drugs and had left. Revived and refreshed by soothing mineral waters, Francis Clareton was holding court where he lay on an overstuffed sofa in his suite. Sometimes he would use the contents of his personal diary to emphasis a point in a reedy voice. He knew better than anyone his brother's weaknesses. He said now, "Remember, dammit, I'm not dead yet. This could go into remission."

"Then you're totally against pulling out of here. Think about it, Francis." Rising, he stepped to gaze out a window. "We can head down to Havana, stay there until you overcame this."

"This basin is tailor-made for us. But not if we repeat the same mistakes we made down in Colorado. I expect we won't."

116

"What you're saying is that I made most of those mistakes."

"You're headstrong with too much of a temper. I've overlooked a lot of things, Thomas. I expect only because we're so much alike. Yes, yes, I've made my share of mistakes."

Turning to gaze at his brother, Thomas Clareton allowed a smile to show. He wore a new brown suit which went well with his tanned face and dark brown hair. Out of deference to his brother's present condition he'd left his cigars behind in his suite. On a table lay some maps and reports and other papers. A glance took in one bearing the name of their new land company. He felt a surge of self-assurance, and he said, "Colorado had its share of crooked lawyers and judges; I expect it'll be no different up here. La Prele wants me to join him down in the barroom."

"How is Jock?"

"He seemed worried about something. But that is his way."

"This La Prele, this Frenchman, is ambitious."

"Oui, I agree."

A wistful smile touched upon Francis Clareton's face. "Those summers in Paris. Long ago and far away. I remember, you were hot-blooded, young, chasing anything that wore a skirt. And I had my moments. As I said, Jock La Prele has ambitions. Which we can use to our advantage. What we can't have now is for you to be too closely associated with La Prele's cutthroats. As you will have to assume some of my duties."

"I know," Thomas sighed, "and don't worry, I'll make no promises to La Prele. Will you need anything?"

"Send in the nurse. Tell me, what did you have to pay her to have her come along?"

On his way to the door Thomas threw back, "Money isn't everything."

Lydia Reinhold was waiting where he'd left her, seated in a chair in his suite. She rose as he crossed to a desk and opened a humidor to take out a handful of cigars. He went back to her and laid a hand on her cheek, her hand came to rest over his. She was quite different from the bar girls he preferred. She was a completely honest woman, and he didn't quite know how to deal with this, or with her. But that she loved him, for the moment, was all he needed to know.

"My brother wants to go to bed."

"He seems to be in better spirits," she said.

"You know I care for you a great deal."

"What about Simone?"

She knew he'd been sharing Simone Jules's bedroom, and he felt no remorse about that; no woman had ever lay claim to Thomas Clareton's heart. "That's over now that we're here. Simone knows that. From now on it'll be strictly business between us. Look, Lydia, I can't promise that I'll ever love you. Perhaps I will, later on. But with my brother ailing, and this new land venture . . . you understand."

"I'm a patient woman, Mr. Wolcott. Something I've inherited from my mother's side of the family." She brought her hand down. Then she stepped over and opened the door and left the suite.

When Thomas Clareton entered the barroom, he found it to be a favorite watering hole for the business-

118

men of Old Thermopolis. Sprinkled in amongst men wearing suits were a few cattlemen, salesmen, and, idling at the bar, one sharp-eyed gent he took to be a gambler. Passing along the bar, he weaved through the tables and eased down at one occupied by Jock La Prele. They shook hands while exchanging appraising glances.

"How's your brother?"

"Bad." He bit the end from a cigar. "Now let's hear it, the bad news."

"You read me pretty good, Mr. Wolcott."

"I should, after all we've been through together."

He filled both shot glasses, and set the bottle down before saying in a soft undertone, "No sooner does Pike Gear pull in than he's involved in a shooting." On the table lay a copy of the *Basin Gazette*. The lead story told of the stagecoach holdup and killings. The story on the shooting of rancher Lon Holter was relegated to a couple of lower columns.

"You mean Gear shot this rancher? I can't believe the man's stupidity. We've got to get rid of him."

"The rancher just got caught in a crossfire. Seems Deal Calloway's luck is still holding."

"The name rings a bell."

"He rode with us. Until we caught him tryin' to help that U.S. marshal."

"Yes, Calloway." Thomas Clareton seemed lost for a moment in his remembrance of that night. He scratched the tip of the wooden match against the edge of the table, and in the sudden flare of light his mind's eye could make out in vivid detail the hungry flames devouring the flesh of that lawman and the man's horrific screams going on and on until he died. The other one, the betrayer, had managed to break away. Just before the flames had eaten down close to his fingers he lit the cigar. Then he dropped what was left of the match into the ashtray and speared La Prele with a pondering gaze. "So he made it up here. But are you sure it's the same man?"

"It's him. Was me, I'da changed my name; seems Calloway ain't all that swift. His face was scarred by that hot tar. Yup, it's Calloway."

"He knows everything."

"I imagine."

"Kill him."

"Can do, but first we've got to find him again."

"I don't want complications, dammit, Jock. He'll be one of our first priorities."

Clareton reached for the newspaper. "This stagecoach thing, more problems. I don't like it."

"You're thinkin' as I am that some of our men pulled this job. They won't admit to it if they did, you know that." Succinctly La Prele detailed how he'd gone along with the manager of the Birdseye stage station in search of the stagecoach, and told all about the letter he'd written and given to the sheriff of Big Horn County. "This banker's wife is a sister to that dead U.S. marshal. They don't know that up here or care. All they want to do is find and hang those killin' everyone aboard that overland stagecoach. Which in this case'll be the Cleo Blaine gang. And Calloway, I don't figure him, as I said, to be too swift. He keeps hidin' out here in the basin we'll come across him—and if he pulls out, so much the better."

This time Thomas Clareton refilled their shot glasses. As he did, his eyes were filled with a new appreciation for Jock La Prele. He recalled the cautionary words of his brother, that La Prele had ambitions. This didn't matter to him, for he knew just how deadly efficient the gunfighter could be. When Francis was scheming over his ledgers, he'd been out with La Prele in the killing fields. Greed, lust, deadly ambitions—these were the things he'd lived with. And if it meant sharing part of this operation in order to make a profit out of this, he could bend a little. But let Jock La Prele prove to be overly ambitious—

"Jock, I'm going to redefine your responsibilities. My brother, he'll still be there, but in a limited role, I'm afraid. But his illness forces me into the role of administrator. You'll be completely in charge of the field operation. Say, for a third of the profits."

"No strings attached?"

"Within reason, yes. I feel to keep the law at bay we must use less violent methods."

La Prele grunted over the rim of his glass. "That'll be like trying to retrain a den of sidewinders."

"Remember, I'll still be in charge."

"Hope it won't be like Lee was at Gettysburg. But I got no argument with that. These spreads around this cattle town seem like good starting points. Calloway could be working for one of these ranches. And if he is, this time he's going down."

Ten

Much to the relief of Deal Calloway there weren't any storms or cold snaps during spring calfing. It was different bearing responsibility for a cattle ranch, not only the herd but the men and horses. Before he realized it they were in the midst of spring branding. To set this off, they'd combed through the draws and rolling land making up Lonetree, to bring in Lon Holter's eight hundred head of shorthorns and mixed stock. They'd missed a few stragglers, as was the case every year, while sprinkled with the herd milling about on the herd ground just east of the home buildings were cattle with other brands than Lonetree's.

Culling out these strays proved to be no problem. These cattle were brought in and placed in one of the corrals. Most of these strays belonged to Count von Lichenstein's Pitchfork Ranch, and when time availed itself he'd trail the strays over there. There was always some griping from the hands, their way of taking it out on saddle sores or the weather, and this spring it was over the cooking, a job that Marge Holter had always supervised. There were three new hands, and to them chow was chow, but men who'd been on for any length of time out here at Lonetree were sorely disappointed that Marge was gone. Along with this there was the worry over bossman Lon Holter.

This day it was warm and getting warmer, climbing into the low seventies. Two big branding fires were going. The men tended the fires and the hot branding irons, sweating from the intense heat of the crackling flames. The way it worked there were two men at each fire, a roper dragging in a calf and holding there with his riata still taut around the calf's neck while one of the hands would grab the tail and use his legs to hold the calf's legs apart. If it was a bull calf, Deal Calloway would decide if it was to be castrated, as every year a handful were to be set aside as breeding bulls.

On this occasion the man astride the roping horse was Mort Elkol, and he made this sage observation, "Yup, this is the time of year bull calves change their minds from ass to grass."

"You're all heart, Mort," said Deal, as he made the decision to have the calf castrated.

First one of the hands would earnotch the calf, then he'd use his knife to cut open the sac and thus remove the testicles. From there he'd pull out of the fire a hot branding iron and slap the Lonetree brand on the right flank of the calf. Then it would be released, to go away bawling in search of its mother.

There'd been nothing sarcastically sadistic about the remark uttered by Mort Elkol. Branding and the other attendant miseries suffered by newborn calves was part of their way of life. Rarely did a bull calf escape being castrated. The purpose of this was to help put more

123

weight onto the animal as it grew. A ranch could keep only so many bulls.

The branding consumed two days and the morning of a third, and as the day warmed, Deal gave the order that brought the herd into motion, but away from the higher ground and onto land lowering into the basin. Further out, the herd would be split up and began grazing, a summer-long process that would fatten them up again. He'd made Elkol his second-in-command, and together they came in on one of the corrals, where Elkol held to the saddle as Deal dismounted.

"It's been a long spring, Deal."

"Too long, it seemed. When the herd is scattered out, Mort, set the men to checking the fences. I expect a lot of barbed wire'll be down. Never liked the stuff myself."

"A necessary evil. When you write to Marge and Lon again, tell them hello for me. I'm glad Lon is coming out of it."

"Some," Deal said as he turned to watch one of the hands detaching himself from the flank of the herd and heading into the buildings at a fast canter.

"Some riders coming in," the hand announced. "A woman and three others."

"Thanks, Cal," said Deal, as he looked at Elkol again. "You'll be in charge when I head over to Meeteetse for that meeting."

"Maybe you could take our cook along and fetch back someone else."

Deal laughed and said, "Beaver's cookin' isn't all that bad."

"Now why do you suppose, Mr. Calloway, they call him Beaver? Not because of them buck teeth either. I swear, you gotta have teeth like one of them furry critters to eat what he throws at you. At least when we're out there hazin' out the cattle to summer range I just might draw a bead on some mule deer."

"They'll be thinned out this time of year."

"But not as tough mangy as what Beaver Tullock's been feedin' us." He left a grin behind as he reined away.

And Deal Calloway, after casting a searching look at four horsemen working their way around the departing herd, began unsaddling his bronc. The frenzied activities of calfing and now spring branding and just running Lonetree had occupied the bulk of his thoughts. He expected a man got used to it. During the days which always stretched from well before sunup to a couple of hours shy of midnight he'd mulled over this notion of him actually taking possession of Lonetree. The last letter from Marge Holter had mentioned it again. If anything her mind-bend to this idea was stronger than ever.

"If she only knew more of what I'd been," he lamented upon turning the bronc into the corral. He set the saddle he held in his left hand on a corral pole along with the blanket. If only, his thoughts went on, there'd been some direction to his life during the years he needed just that. But when you were turned out at fourteen, to drift wherever the wind took you, a helluva lot could go wrong. And it had, but at the time the bitterness in you overruled good judgement, until the time came where you were hung with the brand of high rider. And Deal was finding out that shedding this brand was a painful experience. For no matter what you did or where you went, you couldn't shake loose of some damned bad memories.

The Holters' dog, a collie named Skipper, was out tailwagging to meet the incomers. They'd noticed the lone cowhand turning his horse into the corral, and they veered their mounts in Deal's direction, at a walk. Being out here away from strangers had caused him to forget about his disfigurement of face, and this, along with his customary wariness, brought Deal's guard up. The woman was out front, the span of a horse, her eyes stabbing out at Deal's face, and he held there returning her gaze. It registered that she was kind of comely. Then she was in close, and smiling.

"Mr. Calloway—"

She's the same woman, he realized, who'd been after that outlaw he'd gunned down up on Washakie Needles. He said warily, "Yes, I'm Deal Calloway. Mr. Holter isn't here right now, ma'am."

Easing out of the saddle, she let the reins drop and came in closer to hold out her hand. "It took me a long time to find you, Mr. Calloway. Sheriff Cowley gave me your name. You see, I want to thank you for trying to help my brother."

Deal found himself reaching to shake her hand as he said uncertainly, "Your brother?"

"He was a U.S. marshal working out of southern Colorado. Marshal Ray Webster. I found this out from an outlaw just before they strung him up, away down in Alamosa."

Then she told Deal her name was Cleo Blaine, and she told him the name of the outlaw, but the man's name caused no stir of recognition. As she stepped up to the corral with Deal alongside, she went on to narrate the tale the outlaw had told her of the night U.S. Marshal Ray Webster was murdered. "Mr. Calloway, I'm

126

not concerned that you rode with these killers. But why did you try to help my brother—"

"I . . . I reckon I was trying to make a clean break. We'd just pulled another raid. Were headin' back to Saguache, when I stumbled upon your brother. He'd a died if I just rode on. Afterwards, ma'am, it was just bad luck blundering into those rawhiders. But when bad luck's all you've known . . ." He looked at her companions. "That big man on the roan, is he your brother?"

"Yes, Dave's the only brother I've got left."

"So, you've found me, Mrs. Blaine. It isn't just me that brought you up here."

"They're gathering again, Mr. Calloway. The man you killed up there, Ridley, he was one of them. They tried to take you out down at Old Thermopolis. Between us we can see that justice is brought to the Clareton brothers and the rest of these scum."

Propping a boot on a lower corral pole, Deal tucked a hand in a back pocket of his worn Levi's. From where he stood he took in Washakie Needles fanging up at a mellow blue sky. She stood to his right, taking in the burn mark on his face, compassion for this man pursing her lips. Sheriff Elmo Cowley had told her that Calloway was a hard man to get to know. Could what had happened to Deal Calloway down in Colorado have taken the fight out of him?

"Are you going to this meeting over at Meeteetse, Mr. Calloway?"

"Expect to."

"This thing began last summer. These . . ."

"Mrs. Blaine, I know all about these land agents. I expect you know all about what happened down in Colorado too. That the Claretons had fifty, sixty guns taking out after sodbusters and ranchers and small settlements. Now, like the devil being released from the bottomless pit, they're coming into the basin. Sure, I want to even the score. Especially for what happened to the man who owns this spread, Lonetree. For your brother, Ray. But right now I've got a ranch to run, Mrs. Blaine."

Riding in closer, Dave Webster's saddle creaked as he swung down. "We understand, Mr. Calloway. I know you tried to save my brother. He was just doing his duty as a federal lawman, knew the risks."

"You folks, I figure, aren't about to let go of this. Can't blame you none." Deal nodded at the galvanized water tank over by the windmill. "Your hosses need watering. Even if you plan to head back to Meeteetse, it'll be long after dark before you pull in."

"Are you asking us to stay overnight?"

"Mrs. Blaine, you've come a long way—out of Oklahoma. I'd like to unload what's been on my mind. And not just about your brother. It isn't a pretty story."

"But one I want to hear. And about the men we're after, all of that too."

Meeteetse was an old-time cattlemen's town located in Greybull Valley along the river of the same name. In the early 1880s a post office was established, and soon other buildings were scattered about a crossroads, one road pushing in west from Pitchfork, another from the southern end of the basin to continue on past Meeteetse where a few miles northerly the road forked. From here one branch led to Cody, the other angling along the river looping northeasterly.

An old, pink stone building, the Merchants Bank,

stood on the west side of the road and not all that far from the junction. It was a quiet town, and it took pride in that. And except for Sunshine, it was the only town in the southern reaches of Park County. The trouble they'd had last summer was one reason Sheriff Elmo Cowley had opened up an office, and he was in Meeteetse when word came that Lon Holter had been shot. A day later he learned about those stagecoach killings, the job being pulled by the notorious Cleo Blaine gang, according to a letter Cowley had received from Big Horn County Sheriff Rollie Herslip.

Anger rankled at Elmo Cowley as he made his way toward the Plains Hotel huddled under shading trees. Idlers liked to set and pass the time on the benches strewn under the trees and in front of buildings. He knew about all of them, and would generally pause to exchange a few words. But all that played in Cowley's mind was of his being suckered by this woman claiming to be from Oklahoma.

This Cleo Blaine had really set him up, wrangling an invite to go along when they'd chased that bank-robbing outlaw up onto Washakie Needles. She'd been in on that bank job, and as Cowley sized it up, Bat Ridley had made off with the loot. Only he didn't have any of the bank's money when he'd been killed, which left Sheriff Cowley with the suspicions that more than Ridley and those with Cleo Blaine were a part of her gang.

Cowley'd just left Hoskins Livery Stable, going there an hour earlier to find the woman and her bunch had gone someplace and still weren't back. He entered the lobby of the Plains Hotel, to find the same pair hunched over a cribbage board and Dad Webber still behind the counter. Webber was a stoop-shouldered and florid-faced man whose hair took to turning gray when he was in his late twenties. He owned the hotel, and had vested interests in a couple of other local businesses, in a large part because he had eight children, with his wife expecting again. And he was on the town council.

"Nope, Elmo, no sign of them. Mrs. Blaine did say they'd be back around supper time."

"Mind if I check out their rooms?"

Webber shrugged with his shoulders as a man came through the open lobby door burdened down with a valise and some posters tucked under the other arm. Then the hotel owner said to Cowley, "Check them out if you want—the back three bedrooms on the second floor. But Mrs. Blaine involved in that stagecoach holdup . . . just doesn't set right."

Sheriff Cowley palmed the room key as he glanced at the newcomer, then Cowley headed up the staircase, leaving Dad Webber to open the register on the counter. "Let me introduce myself," the newcomer said as he set the valise down. "I'm Bracy Hume, and I'm here on behalf of the Continental Divide Land Company."

"Must cost plenty to print up fancy posters like that."

"We are a quality company, my good man. And you are?"

"Just call me Dad. Yup, I suppose you can tack one of those up—over there by those calendars. How long will you be staying, Mr. Hume?"

"Indefinitely," came the Euchre Kid's cheery response. "We have plans to headquarter out of your fair city. That big building just down the street, can you perchance tell me who owns it?"

"Repossessed by the bank." Dad Webber studied the wording on the poster backgrounded by a jagged line of

130

mountains. "After ranch property. Not too much for sale in these parts, Mr. Hume."

"You never know about that. Here's twenty dollars for starters. Since this is the only hotel in town, I want to reserve rooms for my associates."

"Reserve—there ain't exactly been a rush to get at the rooms in my hotel. Three or four, yup, we can handle that. An' the banker's name is Grover Farson; unless you've got upfront money don't bother sashaying over there."

As the land agent went up the staircase, Dad Webber rubbed a hand at the nape of his neck, turning to pick up a folded newspaper from others mildewing in a wicker basket. Litter covered the desk he used to do his tallying, but otherwise the lobby had a neat appearance, with sunlight punching through the clerestory and lower windows. He unfolded the newspaper before him on the counter, the latest issue of the *Basin Gazette*.

It didn't say it in the articles he pored over, but he just couldn't believe Sheriff Cowley's accusations that Mrs. Cleo Blaine was involved in that stagecoach incident. Last Thursday, he mused, trying to pinpoint in his mind if that was the night Mrs. Blaine and her traveling companions had lingered over supper in the hotel dining room. But with his wife about to have that baby, and a bunch of other worries tugging at him, part of them his brood of eight younkers, Dad Webber wasn't all that sure. He looked up as Sheriff Cowley reappeared. The sheriff tramped down the staircase and tossed the key over.

"Who's your latest guest?"

"Some land agent. Find anything?"

"Just get word to me when they show up." Cowley

was going to add to this, but tugging at his hat he strode out of the hotel. He didn't want to share with Dad Webber the fact he hadn't found anything in those upstairs rooms tying the present occupants to any robbery. He'd never been a good judge of character when it came to women, but even with that letter from the sheriff of Big Horn County over there on his desk, he'd been holding part of his judgement of Cleo Blaine in reserve. Her story about chasing down the outlaws responsible for murdering her brother rang true—as did a lot of things about the woman.

Tracking back, Sheriff Elmo Cowley remembered that it had taken him a good two days to make that long ride down to the Birdseye stage station. Riding that far made no sense, unless someone had been tipped to a large gold shipment carried by the stagecoach. Nope, he finally surmised, that letter from Sheriff Herslip or no, there simply were too many loopholes in this affair. But one thing Cowley knew, that if Cleo Blaine returned to Meeteetse, and she didn't have an alibi for the night of those killings, he'd herd the lot of them over to the town lockup.

As the evening wore on Deal Calloway began to piece together the names, places and past events of those bloody days down in Colorado. When he wasn't quite sure about the sequence of certain occurrences involving gunplay, Cleo Blaine would fill in the missing gaps. Or her brother Dave would throw in something. He knew that he wouldn't want either of them dodging his back-trail.

He looked about the spacious living room in the log-walled ranch house, which was filled with mementos the Holters had collected over the years. Somehow it didn't seem right being in here; ever since coming back Deal had confined his activities in the house to the kitchen and one of the spare bedrooms. In a way too, he had come to realize, Cleo and Marge Holter weren't all that different. The lives of both women had been forever changed by that killing pack of scum led by the Clareton brothers.

Despite the lack of makeup, Cleo Blaine, with her deeply tanned face, was a handsome woman. She was slimly erect, and from the way she moved gave evidence of spending a lot of time saddlebound; she had the easy grace of the outdoorswoman. She had spoken of her banker husband, just enough to let Deal know Justin Blaine was coming out here. The others who'd come with Cleo had drifted out to the front porch. The flaring of a cigarette told Deal they were still out there, and he looked back at Ray Webster.

"Quite a few of those I rode with are dead. Maybe they're the lucky ones."

"Outlawing is a tough way to make a living, as you've told me, Deal. Like you said, sometimes it just works out a man goes wrong."

"Up here there's a different way of life than down in southern Colorado," said Deal. "More Spanish down there, an easier lifestyle. You said, Cleo, the Claretons were con artists ..."

"They are wanted over in England. Along with Colorado having claims on them." Cleo rose to step up to the fireplace, where she picked up the poker and stirred what was left of a large hunk of wood. She unpinned her hair so that it tumbled around her shoulders, and then her brother stood up to say he wanted some fresh air, and he found the front door. When she set her eyes upon Deal coming to his feet and moving over, they were smiling, trusting. "I know, Deal, what you've told us has been eating away at you, holding it in all these years, I mean."

"How can the four of you . . ."

"Have a chance against these killers? There just might be the two of us. Cholach and Wardell have discussed pulling out for home."

"What did Sheriff Cowley say about all of this?"

"Didn't say all that much. That land agents are always coming into the basin. Now how about you, Mr. Calloway?"

"I was pulled into this after what happened down at Old Thermopolis. Maybe even before over what happened up on Washakie Needles. You'll be in harm's way, Cleo, if the Claretons bring in a dozen or so of these rawhiders. That happens, you look up Elmo Cowley right quick. I'll be in next week, to Meeteetse."

"I'll be looking forward to seeing you again," she said quietly, and then, unexpectedly, Cleo Blaine brought her lips to his cheek, murmuring, "Thank you again, Mr. Calloway." Then she smiled good night and went up a hallway.

Later on that night and after everyone else had gone to bed, Deal went outside and took an ambling and restless walk by the corrals, and with a few horses whickering at him. He was hoping that Cleo's husband could talk her into returning to Oklahoma City. For if they were gathering he expected Jock La Prele would be their leader. And La Prele didn't give a damn if a woman or a child got lined up in his gun sights. The other problem would be convincing Sheriff Elmo Cowley about the impending danger, and if that meant Deal would have to reveal his shady past to Cowley, that would be the way of it.

"Maybe it'll mean I'll never own Lonetree ... but seems there's no other way."

Eleven

"Miss Reinhold, these drugs can induce a man to say most anything."

She continued on with the doctor to the door of the suite, not wanting him to leave. She said, "The last two nights Mr. Wolcott has been out of his head. Then he comes out of it."

"Into moments of lucidity," finished the doctor. "He's dying. But even so, he needs those drugs to help combat the pain. It isn't a pretty thing watching someone succumbing to cancer. About the only merciful thing is if he would fall into a coma—when he does it will only be a matter of hours." The doctor let himself out.

No sooner had the door closed then the pain-racked voice of Francis Clareton pierced out of his bedroom, and she hurried there, only to find that the morphine had taken effect, for he'd fallen asleep. She pulled the coverlet over his arms. For a while she gazed down at him, turned now to lift a window drape aside and stare up the street at the building Thomas Clareton had rented. Daylight was just fading away. Main Street on this Thursday spring day was not all that crowded. Out of the building came Simone Jules, heading toward the hotel. She was filling the role of office manager for the Wolcotts' new land company.

"Only their name isn't Wolcott," Lydia Reinhold said through the fears of what she'd learned from the ramblings of the man in the adjoining bedroom.

How she'd been deceived by Thomas Clareton, by his oiled tongue pouring out that someday they'd be married. She caught her reflection in the window pane and took in the uncertainties playing across her face. Too late, too late now, for before the truth began pouring out of Thomas's brother she'd soiled her body by going to bed with Thomas. Little things that had happened along the way and here began tripping through her mind. Mostly those hard-eyed men such as Jock La Prele ... some of those so-called land agents ... what she'd overheard. The man she assumed she loved she now realized had the guile of a snake charmer.

Hours later Lydia Reinhold tore her eyes open, to realize she was stretched out on a sofa. Floating up through an open window came the plunking notes of a banjo, faint, as if the music was vibrating through a closed door. Then she realized what had roused her was the reedy voice of Francis Clareton coming from the bedroom. It came again, mingled in it a threnody of fear and bitter accusations, as the dying man raged on at the ghosts from the past sharing his hallucinations. And despite her own fears of what she'd learn, Lydia Reinhold slipped into the bedroom.

She was glad now that she'd forgotten to douse the lamp on the stand by the bed. For a while she held by the door, unable to approach the bed, fearful of what she'd learn. Then he stirred about, gesticulating with his arms but with his eyes still closed. This was not the time to tie the rubber cord around his arm and use the hypodermic needle to administer the morphine, to still the pain when he awakened. Now she claimed the chair by the bed.

And she said testingly, "Mr. Clareton, can I help you?"

"You railroad people . . . can go to hell." A trice later Francis Clareton's eyes popped open, but they were unfocused, gaping wide, staring at some invisible enemy.

He spat out vehemently, "I told them, didn't I, Thomas. That we had nothing to do with those killings. Well, we didn't, Thomas . . . for it was our land they were squatting on." He became aware of her, his eyes stabbing that way.

"Yes, it is our land," she said hesitantly.

His mind seemed to accept that, and he began rambling on again, opening the floodgates to what had occurred down in Colorado. There was a mind shift by the man occupying the bed, to what should happen up here—more killings if need be, gain control of the land through any means at our disposal, a patchwork of greedy words which broke away when Francis Clareton cried out at some deep inner pain. With this pain came a moment of clarity, his lips working as he dragged in air, and as he cried out upon recognizing who it was that sat by his bedside, "No more, morphine . . . must have it . . . the pain."

She managed to pierce his forearm with the needle of the syringe, and when she was finished, to turn out the lamp before fleeing the room. Then Lydia Reinhold returned to her room just down the hallway.

Slumping onto her bed, she cradled her arms across

138

her chest, and rocked back and forth, fighting back the tears of indecision, the horror of it all. "I've got to tell the sheriff about this. Why . . . why was I so blind?"

In less than two weeks Thomas Clareton had advertisements about his new land company running in every newspaper in the Big Horn Basin. They hadn't done much of this down in Colorado. He didn't care as long as it brought in landowners anxious to sell out. Out of this he'd picked up some parcels of land upriver from Old Thermopolis. The ads had also brought in folks owning land that was damned worthless. Some of them owned acreage in that semidesert country above the Big Horn River alley—somewhere between sheeped-off range and just plain, gray-brown dirt where weeds barely held on. All the same he'd bought them out at rock-bottom prices.

The plat Thomas Clareton stood before detailed the latest additions of land they'd purchased, and acreage his land agents had acquired. So far there'd only been that one instance where gunplay had been needed; the report of this had been brought to him by Jock La Prele. This had happened easterly out along No Water Creek. La Prele had sent Pike Gear and two other hardcases out there, and when the sodbuster swung down on them with a shotgun, according to Gear, there was no choice but to fire back. Afterwards they'd set fire to the tinder-box of a log cabin. When things quieted down Clareton would go over to the land office and lay claim to that parcel of land.

Where down in Colorado he'd employed a small army of gunhands, up here La Prele had suggested that about a dozen would be enough. That made this a long-haul operation, which didn't set all that well with Thomas. But as long as his brother was alive, he would keep it this way. But Thomas Clareton, as he headed for the front door, wasn't honorbound to doing it the slow way. As he had gotten to liking the bloody way they'd done it before.

He had set up a meeting for tonight with members of the town council and the mayor. And invitations had been extended to the county sheriff and to Thaddeus Miller, editor of the *Basin Gazette*. As long as Miller was there, he didn't particularly care if anybody else showed up. Last Sunday he'd taken Simone Jules, despite her vehement objections, over for morning service at the Liberty Baptist Church. Beforehand he'd gotten the pastor aside to quietly announce he was donating a thousand dollars to the school building fund. That morning's sermon had switched to eulogize Clareton so much he could have walked on water. Tonight's gathering would see him pledge more money to fix the courthouse roof. These were acts that went against his nature, but he knew they would serve to keep the law at bay if something went wrong.

"Keep giving like this," Clareton muttered as he came along the curving bend on Main Street and toward the courthouse, "an' that Baptist preacher'll elevate me to sainthood."

Clareton's smug eyes took in a bunch of buggys and horses lurking by the hitching posts, some more buggys just pulling in, lights pouring out of a first-floor meeting room, and fiddle music. No sooner had he made his way into the meeting room than well-wishers were crowding around to take his hat and grab for his hand.

Sainthood for sure, he mused jeeringly, as he smiled back at Thaddeus Miller and said, "Your paper has some fine editorials."

"We try," Miller said.

As someone else claimed his attention, Clareton took notice of the food he'd catered from a local cafe spread out on two long tables, and of some women clustered there, especially the woman with the burnished head of chestnut-colored hair. She had sort of a Mona Lisa cast to her face, but then she smiled to reveal bony-white teeth, a smile that seemed to brighten up the whole room. Early thirties, he judged, and possessed of a gold wedding ring.

"Mr. Woolsey, if I may have a word . . ."

"Yes, major?"

"It does my heart good to see another business open in our wonderful city."

"We will keep our offices here open. Our plans are to set up other offices around the basin. We've been delayed somewhat by my brother's failing health. But tonight, your honor, the first item on my agenda is to help pay for fixing the courthouse roof—leaks something fierce, I'm told. And that woman in the green dress, would you, your honor, be so kind as to handle the introductions—"

She awoke to find lightning glaring into her room, while the crashing cymbals of thunder were just that and not the crazed incantations spewing out of Francis Clareton. With wakefulness came fear, which Lydia Reinhold managed to push away. For there was something that she must do.

Shoving the coverlet aside, she brought light to a coal oil lamp and brought the lamp over to a wall table. From one of her valises she took out a pad of yellow paper and a pencil. Then she eased onto a chair and drew the robe in closer to ward off the night chill.

Reaching up, she ran a thoughtful hand through her hair, bringing to the forefront of her mind the names and places and events she remembered from the ramblings of Francis Clareton. But first Lydia Reinhold brought the pencil to the top of the pad and printed in these words, "IN CASE OF SOMETHING UNFORESEEN HAPPENING, THIS IS THE LAST AND TRUE STATEMENT OF LYDIA REINHOLD, THE CHANDLER HOTEL, APRIL 15, 1878. . . ."

Her statement, a litany of accusing words, took Lydia Reinhold the better part of three hours by the clock ticking on her dresser. Altogether there were nine pages, torn from the pad, folded to letter size. She had no envelope to put it in, so tiredly she wrote that it should be delivered to the sheriff of Big Horn County.

Uncertainty as to what to do next shone in her eyes as she rose, and it showed the anxious way she shied away from a window through which came reflecting light of the passing rainstorm. During the past weeks she'd caught glimpses of a temper Thomas Clareton kept a tight rein on. What to do with the incriminating evidence she'd just composed? Leaving it in her room was too risky.

The safe behind the counter in the lobby came to mind, but still she hesitated, glancing at the clock—it was going on two o'clock. Which meant nobody would be down in the lobby. "I just," she blurted, "can't leave this here. If Thomas comes across it . . ."

142

Then an idea formed. There was a place where she could leave the statement attesting to the true nature of the Clareton brothers. She slipped out into the hallway which seemed eerily quiet despite a distant thunderclap. She'd overheard Thomas say to his brother that in a couple of weeks they'd be leaving to head up north and deeper into the Big Horn Basin.

Coming down the staircase, she saw to her relief that there was nobody in the lobby. Then she was crossing over to the counter. The big, heavy registry book was closed, and she opened it to leaf to some blank pages. Unfolding the papers, she placed them ever so carefully into the registry book, and then she closed the book. They'd be gone from here, Lydia Reinhold was hoping, before one of the desk clerks came across her statement.

Back in her room, she let the worry of what she'd done unwind from her mind. Her father had come West with a wagon train, and he was always preaching to his children of personal bravery and of standing up for what was right. She knew that the right thing to do was to wait until morning and hand her statement over to the sheriff. But she couldn't. Now she had second thoughts. Perhaps she should slip down into the lobby and retrieve her statement and destroy it.

"What have I done—"

The only thing that responded to Lydia Reinhold's fears was a gust of wind rattling the window panes. No, utterly out of the question. Somebody would have to take a stand in order to stop the Claretons. She had some money saved up, not all that much, but enough to pay the stagecoach fare back to Utah. In response to this ray of hope, she went around the bed to pick up

143

one of her valises, which she brought over to the dresser. She began emptying her clothing out of the drawers. "Tomorrow's stage, got to be on it. Mustn't be seen by Thomas."

Lydia Reinhold managed to pack most of her clothing. She stowed the valises in the closet, and then she stretched out on the bed, drained by what she'd done tonight. The lamp was still on, and it would remain so until it ran out of coal oil. After a while she fell into a troubled sleep.

The night was winding down when at last Thomas Clareton left a casino where he'd been playing five card stud and made his way back to the hotel. The night had gone to his satisfaction. He had come out winner at cards; the woman with the chestnut hair turned out to be widowed, and he'd taken up her invitation to come over for Sunday dinner.

His pledges to help the school and fix the courthouse roof were just that. He had given word that when some money arrived from his Denver bank he'd honor those pledges. He had no intention of doing that, though, since his days in Old Thermopolis were numbered.

"These folks are mud fences," he remarked upon entering the lobby. He went past the room occupied by Simone Jules and paused at the next door. The desire rose in him to go in and climb into the sack with Lydia. But first he wanted to go to his suite and freshen up, use some cologne to rid himself of this whiskery tobacco smell.

He went on to enter his suite of three small rooms. He lighted the lamp on the table by the whiskey cabi-

144

net. Then he heard something and frowned at the closed door running into the adjoining suite occupied by his brother. The sound came again, a sort of frenzied cry, and concern for Francis Clareton made him pick up the lamp and go over to open the door.

The bedroom was off to his right. When he entered the room he found his brother flailing his arms about and uttering broken words and sentences. "Dammit," Thomas cursed, "she must have forgotten to give him a shot of morphine."

"Ah, there you are again," said Francis Clareton, seemingly more clear-eyed now as he sagged back against the pillows. More words spilled out of him. His brother placed the lamp on the bedstand and eased onto the chair.

Thomas Clareton listened in growing anger to what his brother was spilling out about them. What about when Lydia was here, he wondered. What had Francis said to her? He glanced at the glass of water and the vial of morphine, the syringe. Then he knew what must be done.

"Francis," he said gently, "I no longer want to see you suffer like this." He knew that his brother was incapable of responding to his voice, but he went on anyway, spieling out soothing words even as he was leaning in toward the bed to pick up one of the pillows. Half-rising, he lowered the pillow over his brother's face and held it down firmly with both hands.

A dying rattle told him he could remove the pillow, and then Thomas Clareton stood up and passed out of the bedroom, where he eased out into the hallway. He carried with him a key that would unlock the door to Lydia Reinhold's room. But his intention was not to make love to the woman. He could not afford to let her live.

Once the key had rasped into the lock he slipped into the bedroom. The lighted lamp showed her stretched out fully clothed on the bed. Just for a moment he was tempted to make love to Lydia. But he brushed this aside, moving in closer, making a fist and striking her alongside the jawline. Then he lifted her into his arms and retraced his route to his brother's bedroom, where he lowered her into a slumped sitting position on the chair.

Carefully, his face etched in stony unconcern, he filled the hypodermic needle with morphine; a fatal dose. Turning to the chair, he pulled up the sleeve on her left arm. Then the tip of the needle penetrated into her flesh. He emptied the entire contents of the syringe before putting the instrument back on the bedstand. The overdose would take effect within minutes, stilling yet another voice that could bring accusations against him.

One of his brother's eyes was open, and Thomas bent in to close the eye with a lingering hand. "You have taught me much, my brother—but now, au revoir from all the damsels of Paris."

Two days later Francis Clareton was laid to rest in the cemetery just outside of Old Thermopolis, as was Lydia Reinhold.

The day after that Thomas Clareton pulled out for Meeteetse.

Twelve

Cantankerous weather, a wide belt of rain-sogged snow, caught Deal Calloway when he was halfway to Meeteetse. It was the kind of snow that tired out a horse more than anything, coming in cold and wet and sticking to the skin. A horse could barely pluck its hoofs out of the foot-deep drifts. To make it even worse the late spring snowstorm was striking in from about the direction he was headed, from the northeast.

The storm had lifted some, but not all that much, and he could discern ground objects out to a half a mile. What he wasn't tolerating was the heavy wet snow angling in to cut at his face and blind him at times. Tomorrow it would probably be clear, and the snow would melt away quickly, but now, with a grimace for a blast of icy wind, Deal reined the bronc to the northwest. Once he'd seen it snow on the Fourth of July out here; that was the way of the high country. That clump of trees yonderly marked the road westerly to Pitchfork. This quick-moving storm, he figured, would hold up for at least until tomorrow that meeting over at Meeteetse, and asides he wasn't all that keen on going anyway.

147

With the wind slicing at its withers, the bronc found it easier going, picked up more spiritedly to a canter on the red ribbon of road. Now that he'd made the decision to overnight at Pitchfork, the shank of his worries centered on Cleo Blaine. She'd left before sunup for Meeteetse, long before it had started in snowing. He'd got to realizing that someone as spunky as Cleo wouldn't be slowed up for long by any snowstorm. That he had opened up to her was gnawing at Deal too, maybe too much so. Like a man keeping on picking away at a festering wound, rubbing it raw, the raw edges of his past a wound that never seemed to heal. When they'd parted, it had been as friends.

A rift in the clouds brought sunlight busting around where he rode, and the faraway haze slipped out of Deal's eyes when he topped a rise and took in what there was of Pitchfork, with the bronc jerking its head up and down and rippling its shoulder muscles to splay away wet snow. Of all the cow towns in the basin this was his favorite, not so much because of the snow-capped mountains tucked up westerly, but due to its isolation. Rarely did strangers hang in for long at Pitchfork.

There were no horses tied out before buildings, and with this snow still billowing down, everyone was keeping inside. If a man wanted supplies he headed for Mason's Dry Goods store, or for hospitality Nye's Peppermill Saloon & Gaming Emporium, but just Nye's to basin 'pokes. That was all there was to Pitchfork, outside of some old weathered corrals and the livery stable, some distance back of which stood a rickety hip-roofed barn. The hayloft doors were always open, no matter what the weather, and had probably never been closed,

148

at least not since Deal had been coming in here. The hayloft pulley was broken. A rope dangled from a roof support and part of the metal pulley and a tin bucket some wag had tied there about midway in the door openings. In a strong wind they got to banging together making a hellacious racket.

Coming in past Mason's he could make out lamplight and movement inside the store, and then he was at the livery stable and swinging down stiffly, his boots sending up tiny puffs of melting snow and mud. Right away the stable door swung open, to have Deal throw a curt nod at Curly Stopes, the hostler, a black man. It wasn't until Deal had led his bronc inside that he said quietly, "I swear, Curly, is that a new shirt you're decked out in?"

Soberly Stopes replied, "Mistah Deal, this here's a marryin' shirt." A wide grin appeared as he moved with Deal along the middle runway, the bronc in between them. Curly Stopes had kinky gray hair framing a long, sad face, and he had long, bony arms. He'd been a fixture in Pitchfork even before Nye's was built, just appearing one day and doing odd jobs until the hostler quit. Along with helping to run the stable, Stopes did blacksmithing and shoed horses. "Yup, I just took my first step, Mistah Deal, o'er that wide an' deep pit called matrimony. Nevah figured I'd do somethin' so foolish."

"Congrats, Curly. Knowin' you, you'll make it work." He began shucking out of his slicker, grateful to be out of the lifting storm and sharing heat thrown out by the horses crowding the stalls, and with Stopes taking charge of the bronc. Removing his hat, his eyes flicked along the flanks of the horses taking note of the brands. They were all familiar to him, as were some of the horses.

"Sorry, Mistah Deal, we're full-up here in the stable. But I'll make shore your hoss gets bedded down propah in the barn." Through a sad grimace he added, "Sorry about what happened to Mistah Holter; but I hear he's mendin' propah."

Deal smiled his thanks, and he said, "Seems a lot got caught like me halfway to Meeteetse. Leave my bedroll here, Curly. As I don't reckon there'll be any rooms left over at Nye's."

"Plenty of hay," grinned Stopes, "up in the barn loft."

"I had the misfortune, as you know, to bed down there one night. A doggoned wind hooked in around midnight an' all I heard thereafter was that pulley abeatin' the hell out of that bucket. Darned near ruptured my eardrums."

"Suppose I could climb up there and cut that bucket loose. But . . . it's become sort of a church bell to Pitchfork. Least that's my notion, Mistah Deal." Turning, he shuffled on to open the back door and went outside with Deal's horse, the door closing behind, and Deal Calloway went up to a front space occupied by a battered old table and some chairs, where he left his slicker and saddlebags.

That bay, the big one with a star blazed in its forehead, sharing a back stall with a roan gelding, belonged to the owner of the Pitchfork Ranch, which bordered on this small cow town. Otto Franc had built the Pitchfork into one of the truly great cattle ranches. Franc was noted as a big-game hunter.

That roan gelding, mused Deal, as he came out of the stable, could belong to Jimbo Rood. Heading down a snow-covered lane toward Nye's, he began reminiscing how Rood had helped out during all that violence down at Old Thermopolis. "Stuck closer'n a burr," Deal mused appreciatively. "Even after Rood found out about me snuffing out that outlaw up on Washakie Needles."

It came to Deal now that loyalty wasn't something you just up and bought at some mercantile store and that he'd done the acceptable thing by using his sixgun. Bolstered by this he came in on Nye's, wanting to find out what reaction there'd be from others he knew once he shouldered inside.

"Like Elkol always keeps tellin' me, you worry too much, Calloway."

Then he was inside and facing curious eyes.

For the last five miles the small party of horsemen had been guiding on a ridge through which passed the road to Meeteetse. Though worry etched her face, which was tilted up to scan the sullen grey clouds casting down slanting snow, Cleo Blaine, like the others with her, kept her horse to a canter. The road was sloppy wet, patched in places with snow, and there'd be clear places where water trickled across to eat away the roadbed. Beyond that ridgeline lay their destination, with twilight closing around them.

The bitter story told by Deal Calloway back at Lonetree still had center place in her thoughts. She liked the way he'd told it straight out, not hedging what his role had been in Colorado. But it was his eyes which had betrayed Deal Calloway, the times when the pain came out naked, and she realized there was a scar buried in Deal deeper than the one on his face. She found she liked him; it was that simple. In her opinion he'd suffered enough, and if it was up to her a lot of what Deal had revealed to her would never be made public. Her brother Dave had voiced the same thoughts, and now she turned her eyes his way.

"I've been thinking, Dave, about home."

"I have too, Cleo. Justin's last letter mentioned he might come out here."

"You know my husband, says things he doesn't mean. Before all of this happened we wanted to have children. A big family; five boys and five girls."

"Reckon a banker can afford it."

She returned her brother's smile. "Our mail should be catching up to us." Now she lapsed into silence as they entered the gap in the ridge, pulling a cloak of secrecy over her thoughts. The truth was that Cleo Blaine didn't want to go back to Oklahoma City. If she could only convince Justin that their future lay out West, perhaps in this basin. She'd gladly trade their home back there for a rustic cabin snuggled in under some mountain range. They'd traveled West before all of this had happened, mostly to the Denver area. Though Justin had enjoyed what he'd seen of the front range of the Rockies, he'd be the one to suggest cutting their stay short and heading back to Oklahoma. When this was over one way or the other, Cleo knew that if she succumbed to her husband's wishes and went back she'd wither and die. Well, she mused, as through the eastern fringes of the cut they sighted in on Meeteetse, she would stand up for her rights. There was also an inward smile for this vision of Justin flooding her mind—stolid, steady as a rock, an anchor on a windtorn day. It came to Cleo again now, with a vague sense of unrest, that when he arrived she owed him the truth, that she no longer loved him. To tell him this . . . no, bury it, for she'd never doubted his love.

"Dave, when we get in I'm heading over to see the sheriff."

"Cowley . . . he didn't seem all that convinced before, Cleo. Is this about having Cowley send some telegrams down to Colorado?"

"Part of it, Dave. When Deal Calloway comes in I'm hoping he'll back us up."

"If not, if the law up here is still skittish about believing us, Cleo, a lot of ranchers and sodbusters will get hurt." Within a mile of the cow town the road straightened up. The snow fell about them in big lazy flakes, though the air didn't have that deep biting chill of winter in it. Trees, which were plentiful among the buildings they rode past, had their branches bowed low with heavy wet snow. Some branches had snapped off, and here and there a tree had been uprooted. The buildings were also sculpted white. The snow muted the sound of their horses as they came in past an outlaying blacksmith shop, and out of this muted white snow horsemen suddenly appeared, in front and back of the incoming riders.

The only one without a rifle was Sheriff Elmo Cowley, and as he was about to say something, Cleo Blaine said, "I was about to come over to your office."

"That's where you'll be headin', Miz Blaine. You and everyone else." Cowley held back on his words when one of his men levered a shell into the breech of his Henry. The sheriff's reproachful eyes went that way.

"What is this?"

The sheriff, gazing at Dave Webster, said flintily, "I'm arresting the lot of you for robbery and murder." He sat

153

slouched in the saddle, but alert, his gunhand empty and resting on the saddle horn. For all he could see amongst the woman and those with her were eyes filled with confusion and uncertainty. This puzzled Cowley, but the facts about these people had been laid out for him by the sheriff of Big Horn County.

Cleo Blaine was aware of a rider coming in from her left and slightly behind. The man divested her scabbard of the Winchester rifle, and she said angrily to Cowley, "I want an explanation, Sheriff."

"The word I got is that you people stopped that stagecoach just north of the Birdseye stage station. Stopped it and proceeded to kill everyone on that stage."

"I heard about that," Cleo came back worriedly. "But you know it isn't true, Sheriff Cowley. That happened last week."

"I expect you know when it happened, Miz Blaine. Killed them all, Dutch Trajon, Diehl, the passengers including this banker out of Oklahoma. Then you dumped the bodies out by the Wind River."

"A . . . a banker from Oklahoma—"

"You ought to know about that too. 'Cause how else would you come to be usin' the same name. Must have picked up on it from papers he was carrying—yup, awful damned bold of you to call yourself Mrs. Justin Blaine."

"Justin, is dead?"

"As you damn-well know," snapped Cowley. Then Cowley was as surprised as everyone there when the woman calling herself Cleo Blaine toppled limply from her saddle to the slop of the street, the horse sidestepping away.

154

* * *

Pick out any civic group in Old Thermopolis, the town council, school board, or the church council over at the Liberty Baptist Church, and they were all lamenting they'd been suckered by this smooth-talking charlatan posing as a land agent. No laws had been broken by Thomas Clareton, at least according to Sheriff Rollie Herslip. But the rankling effect of Clareton's broken pledges were still grist for the gossip mill at local cafes and saloons. In last Sunday's sermon the pastor at the Baptist church had preached on the subject of the anti-Christ.

As for Sheriff Herslip, he was more concerned with all that had happened about this time at the Chandler Hotel. Tied in with this was the hasty departure from town of Thomas Clareton and his associates. Time and again Herslip had gone up to those rooms in the hotel trying to make better sense out of what had happened to Francis Clareton. An overdose of morphine administered to Lydia Reinhold spelled out suicide. But somehow this hadn't set well with Herslip.

At the moment he was in the suite rented to Francis Clareton. The windows were open and the curtains fluttering slightly in a warming breeze. He entered the bedrooms where the bodies had been found, and the faint scent of medicine filtered his way. He'd seen Lydia Reinhold a couple of times when he had come over to have lunch at the hotel. On both occasions she'd been alone, a lovely woman with quiet eyes. Perhaps it was as Simone Jules had told him, that Lydia Reinhold had been despondent over breaking off her relationship with

155

Thomas Clareton. Though Clareton had backed up this story, it rang falsely to Sheriff Herslip.

"Some of those so-called land agents Clareton brought in," he mused as he removed his hat. "And there's Jock La Prele."

It had proved out that La Prele hadn't been a cow-puncher just drifting in looking for summer work. In fact, La Prele, as he'd found out, had a room reserved for himself in this hotel. Then all of a sudden La Prele and some other men packing guns had left town the day after nurse Reinhold and Francis Clareton had died.

Just standing there at the foot of the bed Sheriff Rollie Herslip knew murder had been committed in this room. It was something as tangible as that dark oaken dresser lurking along the wall. It was an invisible presence, the muted voice of Lydia Reinhold. The hurried tramping of boots on the staircase running up from the lobby brought Herslip pivoting around, and he'd barely cleared the bedroom when the day clerk, Otto Guttenberg, was rushing into the suite, stammering, "Sheriff . . . *diese buchstabe* . . . *ich* find in der hotel register *buch* . . ."

"Settle down now, Otto. What have you got there?"

"Diese buch, this letter, I find. I was dusting the counter when I knocked the register *buch* to the floor." He held up the letter he had opened, his mouth working below the thick mustache sagging down around his chin. "She wrote it, Herr Sheriff, the woman who died in there." He came in to hand the letter to Herslip, and then he sank down upon a sofa and used the handkerchief he held to wipe the sweat from his brow with a shaky hand.

The desk clerk went on, "That letter was tucked into the back of the register *buch*. What does it all mean?"

He couldn't take task with Guttenberg for opening the letter. For all the man knew it could have been placed in the register book before he became sheriff. "Lydia Reinhold?" he read.

"May I go now, Herr Sheriff—"

"Yup," he said impatiently. "But keep quiet about this."

Then Herslip's eyes dropped to what he'd been reading, and as he read the first page and started on a second he realized this was a damning indictment against Thomas Clareton. There was a lot here that he found hard to believe—killings, gunhands, stealing land, and with the names of others involved with the Clareton brothers scattered through the yellow pages of the legacy left by Lydia Reinhold.

"Deal Calloway? Mixed up in this?" Yes, there was more, of how a price had been put on Calloway's head by the Claretons.

But now Sheriff Rollie Herslip knew the woman who'd wrote this had been murdered. No doubt, he pondered, Thomas Clareton killed his own brother. Then he came to the name, Jock La Prele, who Herslip knew was going around the basin calling himself Sam Morgan. "Here, she mentions that stagecoach holdup . . . that it wasn't Cleo Blaine and her bunch but an outlaw named Pike Gear who'd been in on it. Then La Prele suckers me into getting word up into the basin to arrest this Cleo Blaine."

He'd read the indictment hurriedly, through scanning eyes, still disbelieving that these brothers could be so bloodthirsty and so greedy. *Colorado,* mused Herslip, as he left the suite and came down the staircase. *A few telegrams down there will clear a lot of this up.*

157

Out on the street Sheriff Rollie Herslip, as he hurried toward his office, was also thinking about firing another wire up to Elmo Cowley. But he realized that what he held in his hand could carry a lot more weight than a telegram. Once he brought the letter up to Meeteetse it could clear Cleo Blaine of those killing charges. And what about Deal Calloway?

Lon Holter's still here recuperating from that gunshot wound. Which is why he got shot, because he chanced to be with Calloway that night. All adds up now. An' I owe it to the Holters to tell them about this letter left by a mighty courageous woman. Coming in on his office, he called out to one of his deputies heading out the front door. "Nathan, tag along with me while I have a confab with Lon Holter."

The deputy had to pick into a trot to catch up to Sheriff Herslip veering down a lane, the deputy blurting out, "Trouble, Rollie?"

"About the most trouble that's hit the basin in a heap of years. Listen up now, as I've got some errands for you to run."

Marge Holter was the first to see the lawmen coming around the side of the house, and she said softly to her husband, "There's trouble whenever Herslip picks up to that chippy a pace. I just hope . . ."

"That it isn't about Deal," he interjected as he pushed up from the cane chair catching shade from an oak tree. He was healing nicely, but every so often he'd catch himself going kind of weak, which to Lon Holter was an extreme irritation, as he wanted to hitch up a buggy and check out things at Lonetree. "Rollie, Nathan, expect you boys came for some fresh buttermilk."

158

"Hardly that, Lon. Miz Holter, Marge, how you be?"

"Tolerable, Rollie. You look all frazzled up. Don't tell me your missus is expecting again?"

Lon Holter reclaiming his chair caused Herslip to drop onto another as he said to his deputy, "I don't care if Big Horn County Judge Cedric Barlow is in a cutthroat pinochle game over at Lindy's—you get him to send out those telegrams. Then, Nathan, I want my best hoss saddled and waiting over to my office. Tend to it now."

Watching the deputy hurry away, Lon Holter said to his wife, "Better warm up that coffee, Marge. And you'd better put some whiskey in it too, that right, Rollie?"

"You'll need that and more after I tell you what this letter is about, Lon. Damnest thing I ever read."

"Then, Marge," he called out to her just about to enter the house, "you'd better put a double shot into Rollie's cup. So, Sheriff—"

He began by saying this letter confirmed his suspicions that both Thomas Clareton's brother and the man's nurse had been murdered. "Your man Calloway's mixed up in it . . . not in what happened here . . . but southerly in Colorado."

Then he handed the letter to Lon Holter, who placed it in his lap and began reading through the hastily scribbled words describing the violence of not all that long ago. His coffee arrived, but he let the cup stay on the wooden table, coming finally to the last page. "So, I gather this is what the woman, Reinhold, was told by a man dying of cancer. I believe her, Rollie, every word of it. More so because Deal Calloway told me his part in it, when we were coming down to Old Thermopolis."

"He did?"

159

"Didn't hold back anything," affirmed Marge Holter. "It doesn't mention in that letter of how Deal tried to save the life of a U.S. marshal. Nor how he came to be scarred like that . . . scarred by these same men."

"What are your intentions now, Rollie?"

"Lon, I'm heading up to Meeteetse. Me and this letter. I know how you folks feel about Calloway, that . . ."

Marge Holter said firmly, "He is the son we never had. Hell, we've all messed up one place or another, I reckon. You know, Rollie, these men are trying to kill Deal. To silence him if they can. You tell that to Elmo Cowley up there, you do that, Rollie, or so help me."

"Don't get your dander up, Miz Holter," protested Sheriff Herslip as he stood up.

"Rollie, obliged for sharing that letter with us," said Lon Holter.

"I was goin' to ask you more about Calloway. But my feelings are he pulled out down there 'cause he just couldn't stomach what was goin' on. Don't rightly know if there's any paper out on Calloway from down Colorado way. This land fellow, this Thomas Clareton, headed up in the basin someplace, and that killin' bunch of his. Well, best get goin' whilst there's still sunlight left."

Turning to her husband as the sheriff headed away, Marge Holter said, "I've been hankering for a look at Lonetree too. We'll leave at first light."

"Well, doggonit, here you been declarin' I ain't fit to travel noplace, and now we're pullin' out on a long buggy ride. You sure I'm fit to go along, Miz Holter—"

She returned the worried grin poking through the beard her husband had decided to grow, and she said,

"You're fit, Mr. Holter. That meeting over at Mee-teetse—worrys me. As that's where Deal is heading. Maybe those outlaws too."

Thirteen

Jock La Prele and his men weren't in the best frame of mind after waiting out the snowstorm in a line shack someplace north of Pitchfork. The guide they'd hired on in Meeteetse, a down-at-the-heels cowhand, had pulled out sometime before first light, all because Pike Gear had used that big pork sticker he carried to carve a hunk out of Slater Green. They hadn't buried Green but just dumped the body into a deep ravine.

Sighting in on what he believed to be Pitchfork, a few miles to the south, La Prele knew it was coming to a head between him and Gear. Except for Soddy Kling holding his horse back because of a loose shoe, the others were fanned out in front of La Prele, jogging their horses through wet prairie grass. The sun was hot and full out, then a cloud would cut across the sun to cut away some of the glare caused by melting snow. There wasn't any wind, and if there had been, La Prele doubted he could have held his temper in check. Though drinking water was plentiful, they'd run out of grub.

The sun was still low to the east, barely edging over

the Big Horns, and closing in on Pitchfork they saw some movement amongst the buildings: a man walking with a saddled horse, two dogs wolfing about a barrel they'd overturned, a spark of light coming from a building.

Pulling even with La Prele, Soddy Kling said, "You sure this is it?"

"The only settlement out this way," groused La Prele. "I want you to play it cool in there, Soddy. Make sure you pay the smithy for shoeing your hoss."

"If there is one. Or I just might buy me another hoss, as this one has too choppy a stride. Dammit, never figured Gear would do that, take out Slater."

"Leave Pike to me." Last week over at Meeteetse he'd wormed out of Slater Green all the details of that stagecoach holdup. Somehow Pike Gear had found out, too. La Prele knew he should have left Pike dead back out in the tules. Over at Meeteetse Pike had finally gotten around to having those boils affecting him lanced. Maybe this was one of the reasons Pike Gear had turned real mean. Words came back from the pair of riders just ahead of Jock La Prele.

One said, "I caught a glimpse of Pike smiling this morning."

"That so? He must'a had a bowel movement."

Even La Prele had an inward smile for this curt rejoinder as he spurred up to come in alongside Pike Gear. From Gear he received a stolid gaze typical of the man as Gear hawked out phlegm. La Prele said quietly, "Place seems quiet enough, but you never know. I expect that hog ranch yonder'll be the only eatin' place."

"You still pissed 'cause I had that ruckus with Slater."

"We're shorthanded as it is, Pike. I know you an'

163

Slater was at odds; long before we came up here. That's over. But from here on I don't want any more trouble."

"That a threat?"

"All I'm askin' is you put a damper on that temper of yours, Pike. So far things are going good up here. We've hooked onto some fair-sized acreage."

"Maybe so. What about this highbrow Englishman— he ain't half as smart as his brother was."

"Which is why I'm cutting myself in for a bigger part of the action. That could include you too, Pike."

"Okay, I'll be careful about unlimbering my hog iron, Jock. Just don't like bein' crowded."

"There's a lot of things I don't like either."

"Yeah, sometimes life is like lookin' up a dead hoss's rear end, awright."

Opening the back door of the livery stable, Curly Stopes took in the eight horsemen coming in from the north to pass behind the barn. He held there, behind the wheelbarrow filled with horse droppings, watching the riders converge on Nye's. "Trouble," he bemoaned through compressed lips.

They didn't set the saddle like 'pokes did when coming into town. Instead their heads were constantly turning to check out what this place was all about. He took note of the fact they were heavily armed, and the horses they rode weren't small like quarter or cutting horses, but big and rangy, such as lawmen favored. He refrained from going outside until the newcomers were in Nye's. Then Stopes trundled the barrow out to empty it by the manure pile.

About an hour later Stopes heard the front door open

from where he was spreading out straw in a stall. Easing out of the stall, he squinted into the sunlight that outlined a man standing by a horse. "Sorry, mistah, don't have any empty stalls."

"I hear you shoe horses," said Soddy Kling.

"I do. Your hoss laming?"

"While you're about it you might's well put on new shoes all the way around. Any of these horses for sale?"

"One back there; back in the barn."

Kling tied the reins to a support post. He ambled down the runway, taking in the horses tethered in the stalls. When he came to Deal Calloway's bronc, he ran a hand over the brand on the horse's right flank. "The Lonetree brand. Who owns this horse?"

"Well now, mistah, I . . ."

"I like the cut of this bronc—deep-bellied, and with them long legs."

"Don't rightly think that hoss's for sale. But, mistah, Deal Calloway rode that hoss in here."

"What's that you said, nigger?"

"That's Mistah Calloway's hoss?"

"I'll be damned," grinned Soddy Kling. They'd been looking for Calloway ever since that shootout down at Old Thermopolis. To have the man here and at their mercy, and not only that, but Kling knew he'd come into a windfall. Once he got word to Jock La Prele, there'd be no splitting the reward money three or four ways. "Where's Calloway at now?"

"If he didn't get a room over at Mason's I . . ." Curly Stopes paused, trying to keep from glancing over at the ladder running up into the loft. He wasn't sure if Deal Calloway had slept there, but he knew that some late-comers had, and he threw out nervously, "Could be

Mistah Calloway slept in the barn—town's awful crowded."

"Whatever," said Soddy Kling around a secretive grin. "You keep quiet about this, nigger, you hear? Shoe my hoss proper too, dammit."

When he was alone, Curly Stopes drew in a grateful sigh of relief. All of his life he'd seen that kind, thrash-mouthed men, bullies when they were armed, someone who'd gun a man down for no reason at all. Long ago he'd buried anger and hatred, for these were luxuries that he couldn't afford, not if he wanted to lead a normal life. Out here he'd gained a certain respect, and a responsibility to watch out for the horses stabled here as if they were his own. He took pride in what he did, and now he took off for the front door, as Stopes knew he had to warn Deal Calloway.

"That man ain't after Calloway's hoss. Nosirree, he wants to do harm to Mistah Calloway. Lordy, I truly hope there ain't any gunplay on this fine Sunday morning. Lordy, be a shame to disturb the Sabbath."

Last night everyone had agreed they'd hold here in Pitchfork until the sun cast the chill of night away, and then head out together for Meeteetse. Some of these ranchers and 'pokes hadn't seen one another since last year, the result being a lot went to bed later than usual. Along with the regular feed over to Nye's, the owner of Mason's Dry Goods store had put up a couple of tables in a display room and would serve a free breakfast.

Calloway had lucked out when he'd gotten the last upper room at Mason's, but had shared it with two other cowpunchers. Ordinarily he would have gone over to check on his bronc, but he knew Curly Stopes would give it the proper care. When he'd gone into Nye's last night, though there'd been a few curious glances his way, nobody had mentioned that shooting incident up on Washakie Needles. The talk was mostly about how Lon Holter was doing, when Lon would be back and the upcoming meeting at Meeteetse.

Though Deal had been running Lonetree, he didn't consider himself a rancher. At the tables were five ranchers and a scattering of hands. Deal confined what he said to Jimbo Rood seated to his left. "Jimbo, do you think this meeting will accomplish anything?"

"For some it's just an excuse to hit into Meeteetse and see a little gaming action. Maybe, I just don't know. Sure, land buyers have moved in, Deal. And like some I know who've had too many dry years, selling out is the natural thing to do."

"Some hang on even if it means eatin' prairie dog meat."

"All they know or want."

Deal looked at his plate that had held a second helping of fries, eggs and beefsteak, then he eased his cup aside and pushed up from the table. "Think I'll get saddled up, Jimbo."

"Be along in a minute, as there's somethin' I want to ask Mr. Franc. You could saddle my hoss though."

"Could," smiled Deal as he left the room, where out in the back hallway he lifted his hat and sheepskin off a wall peg and went out the door. From here he took in the horses holding in front of Nye's. Draping the coat over a shoulder, he began angling around the large two-story building.

When he came out in front of Mason's, he walked

into the sunlight dappling over and around the livery stable. He took another squint-eyed look southerly at the road ranch to find that three men were heading as he was toward the stable, but with the low sun to the east blinding into his eyes he couldn't make out who they were. Now Deal was aware of the man coming out of the livery stable, and of another man holding a gun on the hostler Stopes.

"Far enough, Calloway!"

Another couple of steps brought Deal Calloway out of the penetrating rays of the morning sun and into shadow cast down by the stable, where he drew up suddenly, and then he recognized Jock La Prele. And Deal didn't have to look around to realize he was boxed in, and with the voice of La Prele tinged with admiration when he said,

"You're one tough sonofabitch. You know why we're here."

"I expect I do." Casually he looked to his left at the three men holding within sixgun range, stepped sideways to take in more of them and Pike Gear coming out from behind a shed.

"I told you it was him."

"Shut up," Gear snapped at Soddy Kling.

There was this rancor coming out of Pike Gear that seemed to push away the chill of morning. Deal recalled that Pike wasn't one to waste much time on words. That time in Conejas burst out of the dark edges of the past, when Pike had been in charge of going in to roust out a few Mex squatters, those people armed with just pitchforks and clubs. For no reason Pike had opened up to kill the three men, and then some women before Deal could get in to wrest Pike Gear's gun away. Ever since

168

then they'd had no use for one another. Deal knew in the gunplay to come his first bullet would be for Pike. But now displeasure creased the lines of his weather-worn face.

He said to La Prele, who was standing with his legs spread apart arrogantly, "Leave the hostler out of this."

Shrugging, the gunfighter said without turning, "Hutto, let the nigger go."

"Sure," responded Frank Hutto, but then, with a vicious snarl twisting up his face, he clubbed the barrel of his Colt down at the head of Curly Stopes, and Stopes went down heavily. "Is that what you meant, Jock?"

"Seems the men you ride with, Jock, are just as scummy lice-ridden as you are."

Though La Prele laughed, a killing look came into his eyes.

Deal said, "This is different up here. There aren't any easy pickings as you had amongst the Mex down in Colorado. You bastards tried to take me out down in Old Thermopolis . . ."

"That was me," Pike Gear threw in.

"Figures," Deal said scornfully. "I owe you for what you did to about the finest man I've ever known."

"Too bad, Calloway," said La Prele, "it won't be just you goin' against Pike."

The rest of what Jock La Prele was going to say never came out as a rifle sounded. There is something about the full-throated roar of a Henry in amongst buildings that raises a man's hackles and otherwise gets his full attention. The echoing sound of that single bullet was followed by Jimbo Rood calling out from where he stood along the side wall of Mason's, "Gents, there's about fifteen more like me holding rifles. But just in case any of you scumbags are stupid enough to make your play—"

When Jimbo Rood's Henry belched flame again, the steeljacketed slug punching out of the barrel set the bucket hooked to the metal pulley wheel up in the barn hayloft to dancing and clanging in protest. Though the hardcases didn't know it, this signalled that court was in session on this Sunday morning in Pitchfork, and that the next move was up to them.

Those with half a grain of sense began to lift their gun hands away from holstered guns. Even La Prele took a backward step as he swiveled his head about to take in what him and his rawhiders were up against. Then the snarly, raspy voice of Pike Gear lashed out at the man he wanted to kill, "You damned-well lucked out again, Calloway."

"I don't see it that way, Gear," spoke up Deal, and as he headed toward the hardcase on a patch of ground damp with melting snow, the sun angling at him and throwing his shadow westerly toward the encircling mountains. "You know, Gear, this is your lucky day."

Confusion swept the anger from Pike Gear's face as he said, "What the hell d'ya mean . . ."

"Don't you get it, you backshootin' bastard? We get to go mano el mano; like you did to that Mex woman down in Trijuilo—only it proved out she had the clap."

Pike Gear looked to the others with him for help, and over at Jock La Prele. "It wasn't just me," Gear said desperately. "Soddy and . . ."

"Damn you," cut in Soddy Kling, "I outta kill you myself." He stabbed a glance at Deal. "If you want to have it out with Pike, it's your play, Calloway—leave me

170

out of it." He unbuckled his gun belt and let it fall to the ground, half-afraid, yet still angry at Gear.

Now it was Pike Gear backing away, hands half-lifted, looking about for the support he knew would never come. And he could see it too in the eyes of the men he rode with, their contempt as the truth about him was coming out. Like the others, he'd shouldered in to slop down whiskey at Nye's. A lifetime of hitting the bottle had scoured his face with mottled veins. But right now he was sobering up to the realization that he was no match for Calloway.

"There's no way out, you yellow dog."

"Sure," Pike said hotly, "I gunned down Holter; damned fool just had to get in the way." He unleashed some more taunting words, hoping it would upset Calloway enough to slow down his draw. "With that scar you're sure an ugly bastard, Calloway. Bet you ain't had a piece of ass in a month of Sundays." He laughed malevolently to cover up the downward thrust of his gunhand, and Gear's gun came out first, though in his haste to pull the trigger the slug spouting out of the barrel merely tugged at Calloway's shirtsleeve.

Pike Gear got one more shot off after he felt the sledgehammer blows of two bullets ripping into his belly and the middle of his chest. He felt himself going sideways, out of control, his mouth rictusing open in disbelief like the gaping beak of a crow. He hadn't expected something like this to happen in this shitkicker of a cow town halfway to nowhere. He did a little toe dance that brought him facing Deal Calloway, whom he viewed through dimming eyes. Pike wanted to say something, and he did, a few chortling words that made no sense. Someone had hazed a small bunch of cattle through here within the last couple of days, as evidenced by the scattering cowpie. When Pike Gear finally fell, it was frontward, as he was dead on his feet. The pity was he never felt his face smacking squarely into a big round heap of cowpie, which splattered up around his head and upper body.

There was a long silence, until one of the ranchers said laconically, "A helluva last meal—but where that bastard's goin' he'll eat more of it. Okay, Calloway, it's still your play."

For a while Deal stood there looking down at the man he'd killed, not really caring as anger still held him in a vise. He turned to look at Jimbo Rood, and then he jerked a finger in the direction of Soddy Kling and said, "Tie him up, Jimbo, and put him aboard his hoss. I'm taking him to Meeteetse." Now Deal pivoted and strode past the hardcases clustered closer to the livery stable. He came in on Frank Hutto, the man who'd used his gun on the hostler, as Hutto protested, "He's just a nigger, dammit."

Quickly Deal reversed his hold on his sixgun to hit Hutto squarely in the face, to have blood erupt out of his nose. Then he grabbed Hutto by the hair and slammed the man's head into the doorframe, and Hutto reeled out toward Jock La Prele standing with his arms outstretched.

"La Prele, you and your men get to your hosses and get the hell out of here, out of the basin."

La Prele wasn't a man taking something as humiliating as this easily, but he was a shade wiser than Pike Gear lying dead out there, and he said flintily, "A man's luck can't hold forever, Calloway. *Cuidado!* This ain't over yet between us."

"You're packing a gun, hombre!"

"Only a fool goes against a stacked deck."

As he watched the hardcases and La Prele come in on their horses and began climbing into saddles, Deal Calloway knew that La Prele was right; they would be squaring off against one another. He could have asked La Prele about the Englishman, Thomas Clareton, but it would have been a waste of time.

"Meeteetse—got this feeling everything's goin' to come to a head over there." Deal holstered his gun and turned to bend down and tend to Curly Stopes.

"I'll be okay, Mistah Calloway," said Stopes as with Deal's help he came to his feet. "Ain't no wind atall; swear I heard the church bell ring."

"Church services just ended."

Comprehension danced in the hostler's eyes when he took in the body of Pike Gear, and Stopes said pityingly, "One of them outlaws—his kind don't evah seem to care what day they die, or spew out death. You killed him, didn't you, Mistah Calloway?" He had a quiet smile for the nod from Deal. "I reckon the Lord'll forgive you. But not his kind."

Fourteen

Cuttingly he said to Simone Jules, "I brought you along because I figured you could keep your mouth shut."

"To murder?"

Thomas Clareton merely smiled from where he sat behind a desk in a back office. He had bought the building from the local bank, to house his land company, and now that he'd decided to stay in the basin, to use it as a base for other business ventures. His land buyers were out giving their pitch to ranchers and homesteaders. And Jock La Prele had pulled out of Meeteetse a day before this snowstorm hit. Despite their differences, he could trust La Prele up to a certain point. As Clareton had found out, the trick was to go along with La Prele's demands. But once his position was secure up here, it would be curtains for the gunfighter.

He relit his cigar, looking through spiraling smoke at the comely face of Simone Jules. "So, you chanced to see me come out of my brother's suite that night. I was concerned about Francis, the awful pain he was in. All

I can say is that Lydia Reinhold was there when I left and you saw me."

"Let's not bandy words, Thomas," she said cagily. "I'm not here to fix the blame on anybody for the past. You're too dangerous a man to have as an enemy."

"As some have found," he said softly.

"You are determined to get into the ranching business—"

"I might be, as I told you."

"La Prele doesn't know a damned thing about how to handle cattle."

"But it's nice to have him around when there's trouble—or killing to be done." He laughed at the cagy set to her eyes, and added, "I know what you're driving at. When does La Prele become expendable?" He rose and came around the desk, where he reached for her gloved hand. "Or you?" Then he stepped to a second-story window and stared upstreet at the jail.

Simone Jules stood up and came to stand alongside Thomas Clareton, where she said, "I have some money saved up."

"You told me that before," he said, and without taking his eyes from Meeteetse's main street.

"I like this land business; reason I came along. Maybe you've lost interest in it now that your brother is gone. But whoever acquires water rights up here will come out on top. Which is what I want, Mr. Clareton. I don't wanna run anymore cathouses or saloons."

"You mean being my office manager doesn't become Madame Jules."

"I'm somewhere between forty and whatever, I'm tough, and damned smart, if I do so say. Street savvy,

Mr. Clareton. Yup, I've seen it all, the last few years the seamy side of life."

"Now"—he turned to face Simone Jules—"you want to grab the brass ring of respectability. I can't chide you any for being ambitious. So make your pitch."

"To clear the air, just because we've slept together doesn't mean there's anything between us. If you get into ranching, you'll want someone young and beautiful and with money connections up here. How you handle this or get your land stocked with cattle is your business, Thomas. As is your past, or mine. Hell, about everybody I've dealt with"—she lifted a cigarello out of her purse—"has a roomful of sins and past misdeeds. Thomas, I want to become partners in this land business. Unlike La Prele, I'm willing to invest money."

"Like how much?"

"Twenty thousand."

He eyed her with new interest. "A lot of money to be packing around."

"My money's tucked away in some Mormon banks."

"Maybe I should"—he smiled—"get into starting up some whorehouses. Twenty grand: that could give you a limited partnership."

"Limited my Irish arse, Mr. Clareton. I've got more money stashed away. We'll cut it right down the middle."

"You're forgetting Jock La Prele."

"Your man. You handle Jock."

"But before we do that there's those prisoners waiting for the territorial judge to set a trial date. This Cleo Blaine knows too much. She's got to be removed, you might say."

Lighting the cigarello, Simone Jules moved with

Clareton back toward his desk, where she dropped the match into an ashtray. As she sat down, she said, "The saloons are full of lynch talk. There are ways to make something happen."

"Is this how a respectable lady is supposed to talk?"

Simone laughed lightly, and easing down onto the edge of the desk, she said, "La Prele, isn't he due back tomorrow?"

"Yes, and I get what you're driving at. Jock and his men can drift through the saloons and gaming joints, stir up what's already been kindled. You know, Miss Jules, I can see where our partnership is going to pay big dividends."

"Shall we go have a drink on that?"

"Dutch?"

"Low card buys."

The ridges were pushing up into crags, the blued Absarokas looming larger as Sheriff Rollie Herslip brought his horse cantering over the road to Meeteetse. Soon he rode through badlands sculpted into jumbled towers, temples, and ruins of pink, red, blue, and slate, which after a while gave way to cedar-stripped ridges, and then Wapiti Ridge and Dead Indian Mountain heaved over a ridgeline like a white storm cloud.

Now Herslip began descending into Greybull Valley. The hub and business center of this small valley was Meeteetse, one of the oldest cow towns in the basin. Unlike other towns lying way to the eastern side of the basin and stretching up north, there were no sheep ranches. Herslip was strictly a cowman, having grown up on a cattle spread down around Rock Springs, but unlike a lot of men used to being around cattle, he didn't have a veiled dislike for sheep growers. And he'd feel a sight better if what had brought him out of Old Thermopolis was just a dispute between these factions. What he carried in his saddlebag, that damning letter of Lydia Reinhold's, was all the evidence he needed to clear Cleo Blaine of those murder charges.

Sheriff Herslip's worry as he spurred his horse into a faster gait on the down-sloping road was the news that a cowpoke had dropped off at Old Thermopolis, that a lot of folks up here wanted a hanging without benefit of a trial. It wouldn't be the first time, nor the last, that justice was sidetracked. He was hoping that by the time he got to Meeteetse a telegram would be waiting for him in response to those that had been sent down to the territorial capital in Colorado.

Otherwise . . .

Dust plumming away from the lower recesses of the road appeared as Herslip came upon blocking junipers and large boulders lurking on a rising hillock. The road was pebbly and drying now that the snow had melted in the ruts. He came around a bend overlooking a meadow dotted with grazing cattle. The dust, he found, was being thrown up by a stagecoach, and he drew off the road and waited for it to come to him, shaping a tailor-made as he did.

He was setting his horse out in the open, so as not to spook the man riding shotgun, whom he recognized now as Sid Placerbill. The horses pulling the stage were coming at a laboring walk. The driver was someone Herslip had never seen before.

He had a wave for Placerbill, a loose-limbed man with shaggy black hair. "Howdy, Sid."

"Howdy yourself, Rollie."

Herslip squinted at the lowering sun and drawled, "Seems you boys got a late start out of Meeteetse."

"The spare stage needed fixing; then just before pulling out we discovered that right rear wheel was cracked. One thing I hate is breaking down between water holes."

"You mean between road ranches, Sid," grinned Sheriff Herslip.

"What brings you up this way?"

"Some prisoners Cowley is holding."

"That bunch," Placerbill spat out derisively. "There shouldn't be any trial for what they done. Just a quick rope and a shallow grave is all they deserve."

"Sometimes that happens," Herslip said upon leaving a quick smile behind as he touched spurs to send his horse past the stagecoach and on his way.

At least, Herslip mused, they're still alive. He still had a ways to go, and it would be late when he pulled in. All the way over here parts of what he had read in Lydia Reinhold's letter kept running through his mind. At first there was some he found hard to believe. But until those hardcases had come into the basin, and Jock La Prele, and these Englishmen, things had been quiet and the way he liked it. Then like a Brahma bull crazed by loco weed all hell had broken loose.

"And no question but that Lydia Reinhold was murdered."

Sheriff Elmo Cowley stood in the shadows of the angled doorway in front of the Absaroka Bank, sizing up the action on Main Street. One of his deputies was in the jail office, the other roaming around soaking up bar talk. And if it hadn't changed any, Cowley knew he just might have to move his prisoners over to the county seat at Cody.

He stood there, a man alone, half-convinced that what Cleo Blaine had told him was the truth. The only trouble was that neither her or the others carried much in the way of private papers to identify just who they were. He went over in his probing thoughts how she'd spilled from her horse when told about that banker being killed in that stagecoach holdup. That her reaction was genuine he had no doubt. But to release her on her own recognizance—she could just take off and leave him with a lot of explaining to do to the territorial judge.

One puzzling thing was her mentioning Deal Calloway and saying that she'd been out to Lonetree. And that Calloway could vouch for her. Deal . . . another man with a cloudy past.

Elmo Cowley was jarred out of his musings by four horsemen coming in abreast from the west. They were headed toward the business places, and in the near-darkness they appeared to be some 'pokes, come in for tomorrow's meeting to be held at Culver Hall, or just in for the evening. Most every lodging place was taken, with some staying at homes of folks they knew or were kin to. Some, he realized, having held to their ranches all through the warming weather of spring, probably weren't aware of those murders. But once they forged into some saloon they'd learn an earful.

Now Cowley could make out there were seven of them, heavily armed men, and he picked out some men he'd seen before. Jock La Prele was one. And the man

180

with a bandanna tied in under his hat was Hutto, he believed. "Yup, Frank Hutto, and looks to be nursin' a cracked skull; hoss probably threw him."

He knew they had come in not all that long ago, to associate themselves with some land agents. Cowley hadn't as yet figured out the connection to that new land company that had opened its doors in Meeteetse.

His thoughts shifted to that upcoming meeting, and to some folks, people who'd been here for a long time, selling out to move out of the basin. He expected that when Pitchfork owner Otto Franc arrived, and some other big cattlemen, he'd be summoned to that meeting. Maybe this new land company, what was it called—Continental Divide—was behind some of the trouble, the news of which had drifted up from southern places in the basin.

Out of a saloon just downstreet emerged Deputy Sheriff Burt Guyman, and Cowley came off the stone steps to begin crossing over in an intercepting course. They stopped along the opposite boardwalk, Cowley saying, "Burt, you remember me telling you about those men claiming to be from Texas. Well they just rode in."

"That La Prele—"

Cowley nodded as he said, "They just pulled around the corner by Farley's place. I want you to keep an eye on them."

"To tell you the truth, Elmo, they look like hombres used to riding the highlines. Okay, I'll mosey over there. Town's in an ugly mood. Maybe we should tell the bars to close early tonight."

"We do that and things'll get uglier in a hurry. I'm amblin' over to my office. An' watch yourself with those hombres too, Burt."

* * *

About a half-hour ago Thomas Clareton had parted company with Simone Jules, who'd gone back to their hotel. Then he'd gone into one saloon, only to vacate it and head for another. Tonight he was restless and curiously remote, as if something was telling the Englishman matters were coming to a head. But why should he harbor such thoughts? After all, the one woman who'd been a thorn in his side was being held over at the jail. Perhaps it was because they still had to find Deal Calloway.

There was one man, he mused bitterly, that had more than his share of luck. From what he'd picked up in Old Thermopolis about Calloway, the man rarely came into town. This was something working in his favor, he realized. But he knew he wouldn't rest until the man was put in a pine box and buried.

Then, just as he was about to enter a main street saloon, Clareton's backward glance picked up on Jock La Prele's arrival, and Clareton strode on toward the building housing his land company business. He went around the frame building and came in the back door, and in his office, he lighted a lamp hanging from a wall attachment. He was pouring whiskey into a glass when the back door creaking open announced La Prele's presence.

When La Prele entered the office Thomas handed the glass to the man, and La Prele said flatly, "We got outfoxed over at Pitchfork. Pike Gear got gunned down too." Then he emptied the glass in a few thirsty gurgles as he moved around to where Clareton was filling another glass.

"Damn, did there have to be gunplay," snapped Clareton.

Wrapping his left hand around the whiskey bottle, La Prele slumped down behind the desk. He tipped his hat back and muttered, "Couldn't be helped as we ran into Deal Calloway."

"What, eight of you couldn't take out one man?"

"Way it goes sometimes," La Prele said sarcastically. "We had Calloway dead to rights. Just that little while until friends of his came out of the woodwork. I don't cotton to facing down men armed with rifles; a heap of them. We was lucky to hightail it out of there."

"We have to go back there and take Calloway out, Jock. Or he'll blow this whole thing wide open."

"We ain't goin' anyplace; that turncoat sonofabitch is headin' this way. An' it ain't just Calloway we have to worry about, as they latched onto Soddy Kling."

"Why Kling? Yes, he was in on the stagecoach holdup. If Soddy gets to talking . . ." He paced to the door, back again, grim-faced, the ugliness of his thoughts flickering out of his eyes. "When do you figure they'll get here?"

"Late tonight, maybe—tomorrow for sure."

"All this lynch talk could work in our favor, Jock."

"Was me I'd set fire to that tinderbox of a jail."

"Not without Soddy in it," Clareton smiled, the whiskey he was drinking warming his stomach, as had those other drinks he'd tossed down tonight. "How about Hutto and, ah, Green, Slater Green, they were in on that job."

"Pike killed Slater. Which leaves Hutto—man's damned tight-lipped. Remember, Mr. Clareton, there ain't all that many of us."

183

"Okay. What I want, Jock, is for you and your men to hit the saloons. From what I've heard so far tonight it won't take too much more to get a lynch mob headed over to that jail."

"Yup, we'll fan the flames of violence. I figure Calloway left Pitchfork shortly after we pulled out. Be here tonight." He heaved to his feet, to spear Thomas Clareton with hard eyes. "If I pull this off, the ante goes up damned high."

"Have I ever reneged on my promises?"

"Promises are like a fart in a closed room. The sound dies away, but the stink remains. I'll handle Calloway. Afterwards, we do some palavering."

Fifteen

About ten miles out of Meeteetse the ranchers and 'pokes riding with Deal Calloway broke canteringly for a side road veering southeasterly. Not all that far away lay the home buildings of Frog Peale's Double D Ranch and a chance to water and rest their horses. Peale was always good for some hot coffee and grub and good conversation. Another reason was that the rancher had three daughters coming onto marrying age.

Even as he went with the others, Deal was debating whether to just keep on for Meeteetse. He hadn't gotten much out of Soddy Kling bouncing along beside him. Tonight the clouds had cleared away, the air was as fresh as it ever got out here and unsullied, to reveal a black sky thick with starlight. During the night it had warmed into the high fifties. Even so, the thin mountain air of this high basin brought a chill to a man. And Deal was bundled up in his sheepskin, and with hoarfrost spilling away from his face and that of his bronc.

They'd held long enough in Pitchfork to bury Pike Gear, not in the small cemetery but out beyond the ravine used as a garbage dump. This was after everyone had learned Gear among others was in on the stagecoach robbery. Deal could remember the anger in the faces of the few who'd gone out to help him bury the outlaw. After a few final whacks of the spade to tap the dirt in firmer around the body, nobody would volunteer to mutter any church words.

"A waste of time," Deal muttered inwardly. Vaguely he remembered that Soddy Kling had joined that killing bunch down in Colorado a week before Deal decided to cut out. The trouble was, there were so many like Kling, drifters, lazy saddle bums who'd got the notion they could take whatever they needed. One bad habit led to another until a man got so hard inside you could see the eyes of the devil himself gleaming out of the man's skull. They'd said that about him, Deal recalled.

From Jimbo Rood, who'd reined back, "I expect we could overnight at the Double D; but a night like this sure makes a man feel good. You get anything out of that scumbum?"

"Claims it was Pike's idea."

"Heard that line before. You want, Deal, I could detour out amongst the tules and pistol-whip it out of him."

"Been thinkin' of that myself." He grinned back.

Now in a soft undertone Rood said, "I killed a man once. Up in Canada—western Manitoba it was. Some Canuck got owly in a poker game and wouldn't admit he was cheating. So he came at me with a Green River; had no choice but to unlimber my hog iron. Being a stranger to that town I left mighty fast. I expect, as it is for you, Deal, killing a man don't come easy."

"Do you ever learn to live with it?" shrugged Deal.

"Remember this, Mr. Calloway, this Pike Gear was

justifiable homicide, killing him, I mean. There was a lot of innocent blood on his hands, as was the case with that other hardcase up on Washakie Needles. Well, we're comin' onto Frog's place—and there's some lights a-showing. Which means those daughters of Frog's will be dishing out some vittles."

"For a man confirmed to a life of bachelorhood, Jimbo, that's mighty changeable talk."

Rood smiled, "You never know."

"I'm thirsty," whined Soddy Kling.

"So's your hoss," snapped Deal, "and he gets watered first. You know, Soddy, you're like the snow melting over in yonder draw. Just like that, you're gone. With nothing to mark the spot where you died. You tell what you know, you just might not be hung but receive a life sentence. As if any of those others get caught, they'd sure as sin spill their guts out about you."

"You think so?"

"Chew on it, Soddy," he said flatly, and as they came in amongst the buildings, where three dogs began circling around the riders as the rancher and his wife and two of their daughters came out of the rambling log house. One of the girls reminded Deal of Cleo Blaine, and he hoped that Cleo had made it to Meeteetse. Then he was riding by and coming in on a water tank, kind of bone-weary, and not looking forward to the rest of his trip.

Only five of them had pulled out for Meeteetse. The rest, about a dozen men, stayed at the Double D Ranch. For about two miles it was rough riding as the road wended up long slopes, but then they were descending into Greybull Valley and coming in on a creek the Shoshone called Meeteetse, place of rest. Beyond that lights from the cow town they were headed for picked up their pace.

Deal hadn't got all that much out of Soddy Kling, and he knew the hardcase had set his mind against telling what he knew.

"You know, Soddy, I've a notion to let you have your pistol back."

The outlaw glared at Calloway, and there was an insolent twist to his thin mouth.

"Then you and me match draws right here. You game for that, Soddy?"

Jimbo Rood said, "Hey, that's a fair deal, you ambushin' bastard. A better deal than doin' some sky-dancing."

"Piss off, the both of you," Soddy blurted out.

Reining in closer, Deal grabbed Kling's shirtfront, and then he backhanded the hardcase, holding the man to his saddle to keep him from falling as he lashed out with more skin-popping blows to the head. "I outta gut and skin you like that other bastard did to a friend of mine up there on Washakie Needles. You sonofabitch, when we get in there, you're gonna rattle what you know to the sheriff. Or you can die right here, Soddy, 'cause we ain't goin' any further until I get an answer." Deal stopped both of their horses, Jimbo Rood and the others encircling to take this in.

When Deal released his hold on the hardcase, Kling spat out blood and trembling words, "Dammit, Calloway, you busted my nose and maybe . . . maybe my jaw. I'll do it, dammit, I'll rat on the others. 'Cause

I ain't got no chance against your draw, damn you, Calloway."

Reaching back for his canteen, Jimbo Rood untied it from a saddle loop, and after uncorking it, he let the cold water trickle over Soddy Kling's head and shoulders. "Bless you, my son, for seein' the light," he said.

"A good waste of water," said one of the 'pokes.

"Gets rid of some of his stink," remarked another.

And from Calloway, "Let's get in there."

All of them held together until they came in on the street and gazed upon the barred windows and doors of the jailhouse. There was some small talk as their horses milled about. Rood and Deal rode on with their prisoner, then pulled up and dismounted by the hitching rack. As they did, the front door opened some and Sheriff Elmo Cowley came outside holding a rifle.

"You goin' hunting, Elmo?" inquired Jimbo Rood.

"It's what I've got in my cells," countered the sheriff. "I'm holdin' those who held up that stage up north of Birdseye station. A woman and three others—woman named Cleo Blaine."

"Cleo?"

He stared at Deal untying the ropes binding his prisoner to the saddle of the gelding, and Cowley said, "You know her? And who is this gent?"

Deal reached to where Kling's hands were bound together with a short hunk of rope, and then he jerked the hardcase out of the saddle. The man fell heavily at his feet, and the gelding shied away. Deal said, "His name's Soddy Kling. This useless hunk of dog meat can tell you who really held up that stage. As he was one of them. Come on, Soddy, pick your ass up and get in there."

"Ain't you treatin' your prisoner kind of rough, Deal?"

"Along with that stage robbery, he was one of those pullin' that ambush on me and Jimbo here, and on Lon Holter, down in Old Thermopolis. You got writing material in there?"

"Some."

"Good. By the time Soddy gets done tellin' what he knows you'll have writer's cramp, Elmo." He brought Kling in through the front door and over to a chair resting by the side of the room's only desk, and nodded to Deputy Sheriff Pat Delsing. Then, turning, Deal said to Cowley, "You're holding Cleo Blaine?"

"Yup, have been ever since she came back from seeing you out at Lonetree. You're telling me she or the others didn't pull that robbery?"

Said Jimbo Rood, "They came into Pitchfork. Him"—he nodded at Soddy Kling—"and a bunch of others. They had Deal corralled over by the livery stable, an' were fixin' to gun him down when me and Otto Franc and some other ranchers horned in. There was gunplay; Deal squared off with one of them hardcases, a gent named Pike Gear. Gear's dead, an' we're here. Back there though, this hombre, Kling, confessed to his part in that stagecoach robbery."

"I'll take his statement," said Cowley. "But the word I got from Sheriff Herslip down at Old Thermopolis was that it was Cleo Blaine. I just don't know, boys." He reached over and placed the rifle back in a wall gun rack. "What worries me is all this lynch talk. I have to say, it all comes down to this gent's word against that of Cleo Blaine."

"I can vouch for Cleo," Deal said flatly.

"You knew her from before?"

"Not her, Elmo. But I more or less knew her brother down Colorado way. He was a U.S. marshal." Deal's voice had a note of finality to it, as if what he'd held in all of these bitter years could no longer be contained in the dark edges of his memory. Suddenly he felt an easing of tension, and he flashed a taut smile. "Nope, those you're holding aren't criminals. But I was one once—"

Now everyone in the jail office realized that an intruder stood just outside the open door, off in the shadows, and had been listening to the byplay of words. The man who revealed himself wore a sheriff's badge and had a saddlebag slung over one arm. He said, "I can vouch for what Calloway is about to tell you. And like Deal Calloway just stated, Cleo Blaine is no criminal."

Cowley blurted out, "Rollie, awful late to be showing up here. Now what's that?"

"The last testament of a woman who was murdered by Thomas Clareton down at Old Thermopolis!"

Sixteen

Gunfighter Jock La Prele and another hardcase were encamped at the Grotto Saloon, which was located a block and a half south of the jailhouse. They'd made the rounds of the other drinking establishments, adding a few words to the anger everyone had for the prisoners being held by Sheriff Elmo Cowley.

La Prele, as he tossed some chips into the ante pile, brought his eyes flicking to Frank Hutto, who was holding court at the front end of the fancy oaken bar. There Hutto was, the nervy son'bitch, clustered in with some cattlemen, as he kept the lynch talk stirring in a cauldron of bile. If those cattlemen ever suspected, La Prele chuckled inwardly, that Hutto had been in on those killings, it would happen right here in the Grotto, Frank Hutto being strung up to dangle from one of the piney roof rafters.

Now the hand was played out, and a local merchant was raking in the chips, and La Prele shook his head in dismay as he drawled, "There's another hand I should have folded."

"Your luck is sure running cold."

"Rather be doin' this than sittin' at home listenin' to the missus bitch about somethin' or other."

A rancher in the game laughed as he caught the eye of a passing barmaid, to order drinks around. "So you're up here hopin' to latch onto some land."

La Prele nodded. "Trying to, all right. But it troubles me when I hear quite a few are sellin' their spreads."

"Why I'm in here," stated the rancher. "Not to sell out, but to attend tomorrow's meeting."

"I've heard about that."

"Yup, some land agents have come in here, into the basin, stirring up things. An' us old-timers don't like it."

When the round of drinks arrived, everyone settled back into the game, and coming onto midnight now business in the saloon seemed to pick up considerable. The shape of a 'poke's hat caught La Prele's eyes, and he realized the cowpuncher had been in Pitchfork during that run-in with Deal Calloway. He filed this away, fanning out the cards he'd just been dealt—three jacks and a deuce and a seven. Any other time this would have prompted La Prele to shove more chips into the pile. Instead he merely flipped a blue chip worth five dollars in with the others and discarded the deuce and seven.

He was expecting his men to put in an appearance. There weren't all that many saloons in Meeteetse. La Prele had picked this one out as a place where cattlemen like to congregate. As he sipped from his glass, the batwings stirred and land agent Matt Segelke came in to wedge a place at the bar. Then Segelke half-turned to look over the large interior. Spotting La Prele, he tipped a finger to his hat. Again someone entered; it was Pony Bob Haslam joining Segelke at the bar.

"You dropping out again?"

La Prele looked across the table and said, "Just might as my mind sure ain't on this game." Now he looked at the pair of cards he'd been dealt, one of them the fourth jack, to which he merely grimaced. "Everytime I get a hand like this, I come in seconds. But what the hell . . ."

"Your raise—"

"Okay," said La Prele, "your five . . . and fifty dollars more . . ."

"You sure got guts," grunted the rancher, as he studied La Prele's face. "Or maybe you're just a glutton for punishment. That'll cover your raise; and sir, two hundred more."

Tipping his hat back, La Prele allowed a slow smile to crease across his face. "This is like investin' in livestock when the market price is below the freezin's mark. A case where a man just can't stop throwin' good money after bad. There, what chips I've got left."

Eagerly the rancher spread out his cards faceup, to reveal he had a full house. Now it was La Prele following suit, and it took a moment to register around the table that La Prele's four jacks had just won the biggest pot of the night.

"Doggonit," groused the rancher. "No offense, but even a blind pig finds an acorn you leave him under an oak tree long enough. What about you boys, you don't suppose Mr. Sam Morgan owes us a drink."

It was then that La Prele became aware that the man who'd just ambled over to their table had a sheriff's badge pinned to his flannel shirt, the man saying, "How you been, Mr. Morgan?"

"Sheriff Herslip, wasn't it? Can't complain."

The rancher exclaimed, "Well I'll be, Rollie Herslip. You lost or something?"

"You could say that. It was Sam Morgan here who helped find that stagecoach after that robbery. Bodies been laying out long enough for the vultures to do a lot of damage. Now I hear the men who did this are jailed here."

"They outta hang the bastards," the merchant said viciously. "Who knows who'll be killed next?"

"Mr. Morgan, despite your taking a lot of my money, let me shake your hand," the rancher said. "I agree with Donnelly here, that they outta be taken out and strung up." The rancher's loud, raspy voice brought a few drifting in closer, and the Euchre Kid and Pony Bob Haslam away from the bar. "What galls me is that Dutch Trajon was one of the finest hands I ever had. Before he took to driving stagecoaches."

"They'll be punished," cut in Sheriff Rollie Herslip. "No good ever came out of taking the law into your own hands. Mr. Morgan will agree to that." He held by the table as blustery talk continued, but then his presence brought most turning away. "One thing, Mr. Morgan, if you've got a minute."

"Sure?"

"Tomorrow Sheriff Cowley will be taking the prisoners up to Cody to stand trial. Figures as I do something might happen here in Meeteetse. Did you ever buy that ranch you've been looking for?"

"Come close, but I'm still looking, Sheriff."

"Take care," said Herslip as he headed for the batwings.

* * *

Despite the damning evidence brought up from Old Thermopolis by Sheriff Herslip, Deal Calloway knew that another lawman still wasn't convinced of the innocence of Cleo Blaine, her brother and the two men with them. But at least they'd convinced Sheriff Elmo Cowley to remove the prisoners from the jail, a deputy remaining there in the office just in case there were some late-night visitors.

Anxiously those waiting on the front porch of Sheriff Cowley's big gabled house kept stabbing glances up the lane running toward Cedar Street. The porch was covered with wire-mesh screen to keep out summery insects, and it had on it some cane chairs and a big comfortable davenport on which Cleo Blaine and the sheriff's wife were sitting. Reflected light came through the two windows and the door. The house was set in behind spreading lilac bushes, and one enormous oak tree dominated the front lawn.

Once in a while Cowley would turn slightly to look at the two men taking their ease in his living room, just to make sure they hadn't cut out someplace. On the porch with him stood Deal Calloway and Cleo's brother Dave Webster. He hadn't been so liberal with the other prisoner Calloway had brought over from Pitchfork; Soddy Kling was locked in the potato cellar.

While one of his deputies was at the jail, Cowley had sent his other one over to keep an eye on the hotel where the Englishman had taken up lodging.

The cup he held was part of a set of chinaware they'd been given at their wedding reception. Not only had his wife Norma dragged out their best chinaware, but she'd gone whole hog for their unexpected guests by using their best set of silverware too, and Cowley was still rankled by this. But that was Norma, liking to see the good in everybody, even after all of his years of sheriffing.

"Calloway, I still can't believe I let you and Herslip talk me into this." Grimacing, he turned his eyes upon Dave Webster. "I have to believe some of this. But until I receive word from Colorado I've got no choice but to hold you. Though your sister Cleo, she's all but got me convinced otherwise."

"Troubles me that those hardcases," said Webster, "are circulating around town spilling out that we should be taken out and hung."

"I do declare," spoke up Norma Cowley, "those taters should be about boiled by now. The rest of it's ready, so everybody, let's go chow down."

Deal waited with Sheriff Cowley as the others went into the house, and then Cowley said, "Herslip should be back most anytime. Now tomorrow, everything seems to be set. I just hope this works out, Deal, without any of those who've volunteered to help gettin' hurt."

"If Jock La Prele falls for it, he'll be out there set in ambush to make a go for your prisoners. I'd rather be ridin' a hoss than in that buggy with Soddy Kling."

"An' I expect Kling won't like it a damned being dolled up to look like a woman. That could be Herslip."

Up the lane came Sheriff Rollie Herslip, and then he was opening the screen door and removing his hat as he stepped up onto the porch. "Took me a while to find La Prele. I left the saloon first so I don't know if he took the bait."

"Got my deputy watchin' Clareton's hotel. We'll soon know. Been a long day, gents, and I ain't et since morning. So let's chow down."

197

* * *

When Jock La Prele slipped out of the Grotto Saloon, it was alone. The gunfighter headed south, toward the hotel, while viewing the jail on the opposite side of the street. He detected the form of a man rising from behind a desk, and for a moment it seemed strange to La Prele that only one lawman was keeping watch over the prisoners. "That Cowley's crafty as they come. Could be he's got others scattered around just in case a lynch mob shows up."

He passed a saloon, where some cowhands were standing out front, and when he veered around them he began angling across the intersection toward the hotel. Then he was going into the lobby; a deputy sheriff taking note of the gunfighter's arrival.

On a hunch La Prele decided to check out the barroom. The room wasn't as crowded as the bar he'd been in, so he was able to pick out Thomas Clareton seated at a table talking to some woman. After a good look at La Prele's face the film of irritation went out of Clareton's eyes. "Trouble?"

"Maybe not. Maybe this time we lucked out." Pulling a chair away, La Prele sat down. His eyes slid to the woman. "Take a hike, pussycat."

"Why, I never . . ." She rose glaring from the gunfighter to Thomas Clareton, who said, "Business, Rose. I'll see you later."

As the woman swept out of the barroom, La Prele said laconically, "Ain't she a bit jaded for your tastes?"

Clareton merely shrugged. "So what have you got?"

"Seems we won't have to stir up a lynch mob. As the

198

prisoners are being moved to Cody. Tomorrow morning sometime."

"What about Soddy Kling?"

"I suppose he'll be going along. And so will you, Mr. Clareton."

"Easy, Jock, that's your job, killing."

"I remember how it was," La Prele snapped back, "that night when we killed that U.S. marshal. You enjoyed it. You enjoyed ridin' along at times when we took out women and children. So you ain't sittin' back up here and keepin' clear of the dirty work. You're goin', Clareton, or you'd better be packin' a gun next time we eyeball one another."

After a while, and as Thomas Clareton glared back at the gunfighter, the realization dawned that he had no other choice.

"Asides," La Prele said to ease the sting of his words, "Deal Calloway will be helping with the prisoners. He's the one man standing 'tween us and paydirt."

A smile gleamed out of Clareton's eyes, and he said, "The only way is to kill them. What time do we leave?"

"Damned early; next three, four hours. I'll be by to roust you."

"Then I'd better catch up with Rose and call it a night."

"Whatever," La Prele said stoically as he rose and left, thinking as he cleared the hotel that after this was over, it would be time to get rid of that woman-hungry idiot.

Seventeen

Even before false dawn was touching upon the basin Deal Calloway had brought the buggy some three miles north of Meeteetse. With him on the front seat sat Soddy Kling decked out in a dark blue bonnet and a shawl slung over his shoulders. He'd been given no choice in this, as Sheriff Elmo Cowley had ordered him out of that potato cellar, and then before Kling realized what was happening, he was told to get aboard a buggy. Now, with the sun about to touch over the horizon, the three men occupying the buggy's back seat couldn't help but throw an occasional smile at the outlaw's unusual choice of clothing.

These three had volunteered to take the place of Cowley's prisoners. If there was an ambush, they'd be the first to come under fire.

After supper was over last night, Deal and Sheriff Cowley had gone out to have a long talk on the front porch. Most of it had to do with Deal, and most of it was about his past. Then the talk had centered upon Cleo Blaine. The sheriff was beginning to agree that she hadn't been involved in any stagecoach robbery. But stubborn as Cowley was, he couldn't let go of the notion a telegram from Colorado could clear everything up.

Out front of the buggy bouncing through some angling ruts in the main road to Cody rode a deputy sheriff, and behind Sheriff Cowley sat his saddle alongside one of the cowhands volunteering to help defend the prisoners. A second bunch of horsemen had left even earlier from Meeteetse, men under the command of Sheriff Rollie Herslip. Once they got out a ways, they'd split into two groups and keep to either side of the road but far enough away so they wouldn't be spotted by anyone setting up an ambush. This was about as well as Sheriff Cowley could plan this, and even then he wasn't satisfied.

He spurred up now to come alongside Deal Calloway, who brought the wagon over some to make room for Cowley's horse on the narrow span of gravelly road. Shadows still clung doggedly to lower elevations. The air was still, and sound carried a long way at this time of day, and the sheriff said softly, "You don't believe there's any wanteds out on you, Deal?"

"Not that I know of. There were so many of us, Elmo, that lawmen done there couldn't get a fix on any particular man. Looking back, hard to believe all of that happened."

"I knew this man rode with them Jayhawkers. That was some bloody, killin' mess. Anyway, he said you just get caught up in it. Like a fever takes over. Which some never get rid of, Deal. Hanging to this buggy like you are, if they're out there, you'll be their first target."

"Don't forget Mr. Kling here," Deal said.

"Even with that bonnet on he's still kind of scrawny ugly," said Cowley.

"Dammit," said Soddy Kling, "I figured I'd get a better deal out of this after I told you what I know, Sheriff. Posing as some woman—even being hung sounds better."

"Maybe the judge will oblige you," remarked Sheriff Cowley as he spurred on to catch up to his deputy.

Astride a mottled grey gelding, Deputy Burt Guyman kept his eyes trained on a rocky escarpment about a mile to the north, where the road curled along its lower reaches. Opposite of that there was more high ground, mostly humpbacked hills that didn't amount to much compared to the mountain peaks westerly. As the tip of the sun appeared it sparked out blinding yellow light that caused both men to squint and turn their heads away.

"We'll be blind as moles and they know it."

"The ambushers. Yup, if they're out there. Got this feeling they are. We could turn back."

"You're calling it, Elmo."

"Beyond that escarpment is more places they could ambush us. Rollie Herslip and his men—just hope they spot them first."

As far as Jock La Prele was concerned, the Englishman had signed his own death warrant. He'd gone to the hotel, only to discover that Thomas Clareton was gone. From Clareton's room La Prele had broken into the one occupied by former madam Simone Jules, to find her still sleep-laden and unable to help him locate Clareton. From here La Prele's raging anger had carried him and the other hardcases out of town.

After he'd calmed down, the gunfighter had selected

one of those unnamed rocky, red-soiled hills overlooking the stagecoach road. Some of his men had crossed over to settle in amongst the lower hills to the east, but in close enough to allow them to use their rifles with lethal effect. The gunfighter's orders were that there be no survivors.

He sighted down the length of the Winchester barrel at a spot where the road dipped to proceed along a long open space, wishing he had the Englishman in his sights. Around him junipers were beginning to rustle to hint of a coming wind. Otherwise, the deep quiet of a newborn day still lay over the basin. The sun would change this, rising more now, edging upward behind tufts of pink clouds. As the day warmed, thermals would form around the mountains, and hawks and eagles would begin their almost daily ritual of riding these rising spirals of wind high over the basin on outspread wings as they searched for prey.

"Well," mused La Prele, "we know our prey is comin' right down that road."

"They should be comin' soon," said Frank Hutto.

Jock La Prele hadn't seen any need to tell his men of last night's encounter with Clareton. He knew that Clareton had some money stashed over at his land office, a heap more spread around in banks and deeds to land in the Big Horn Basin. Knowing Clareton's style, he'd augered it out that the man would find a hole to crawl into, a place like Denver or San Francisco, just until things cooled down out here. Along with this, La Prele had no illusions but that a bounty would be placed on his head, as now it all came down to a case of who killed who first.

The way La Prele had set up the ambush site was

with his best riflemen hiding east of the road, the sun over their shoulders, the men at the road facing into the low morning sun. That first volley of rifle fire would drive those on the road in La Prele's direction, to seek cover in a jumble of rocks below where he sat with his back against the bole of a juniper. It shouldn't take more than five minutes at most to do this killing job. Then, whilst his men closed in to divvy up the spoils, he'd be wheeling his horse southerly back to Meeteetse in time to be there when the eleven o'clock stage pulled out for Old Thermopolis.

"Though I'll kind of miss bein' around that wheeler-dealer—"

"What's that, Jock?"

"Just ruminating about what greed can do, Hutto," he snorted, as to them came from a nearby and unseen body of water the eerie call of a loon. First La Prele took a sip from the bottle of Carstair's Best. Then through a smile in his eyes he added, "When a loon sounds, somethin' always seems to happen afterwards. Won't be long before we sight in on them."

It helped ease Sheriff Rollie Herslip's worries that he was riding with men who knew this part of the basin better'n the palms of their hands. Half of the twenty or so men who'd left with Herslip were scouring the floor of the basin on a course paralleling and east of the stagecoach road. As for Herslip, they'd picked up one fresh trail, which proved out to be some 'pokes joining up with others hazing a herd of cattle Cody way. They'd also come across plenty of fresh game sign, even the spore of a moose coming out of high country in search of fresher grass.

He looked over at Jimbo Rood scanning the varying elevations that guarded the road through a field glass, and with sunlight glinting away from Rood's conched saddle. "Thought I spotted something," Rood said after a while, "but gazing into the sun like this . . ."

"I don't expect they kept to the road when pulling out of Meeteetse. But hooked up with it later."

"At least nobody saw them pull out," commented Rood as he reached back and put the field glass in a saddlebag.

"You know Cowley better'n me, Jimbo."

"We both know he's awful stiff-backed. Worse than one of them show-me-Missourians. At least he went along with this plan of Calloway's."

"I don't know as how I'd be holdin' to that buggy like Calloway and those others are—when it all hinges on us spotting them ambushers first."

A low whistle from the point rider brought them spurring through sagebrush and to the western bank of a swollen creek, although some of the riders held out where they were, reining in to keen their eyes at what was happening. Herslip, Jimbo Rood and rancher Otto Franc noticed the fresh hoofprints sunk deep in the muddy bank, and more on the eastern side of the creek.

"Got to be them," said Herslip, and he waved everyone in as he brought his bronc plunging after Rood and Otto Franc, just about in midstream of the narrow creek that was bringing snowmelt waters out of the Absarokas.

The front riders, those who'd crossed, held a short distance away from the far bank. The water had splashed up to wet their clothing and empty gunbelts, but the way the sun was clearing some low clouds, it wouldn't take long for them to dry out. As they watched, one of the tailing riders got dislodged from his saddle but managed to cling to the reins, and then he was splashing to his feet in shallower water and shivering through a sheepish grin. He led his horse up the low bank and joined the others.

"Fust time you crossed water, Maury?" a cowhand threw at him.

"Just what he needed, a bath." Jimbo Rood looked at Sheriff Herslip. "Those hombres are angling for that high ridge this side of the road; I figure three miles away."

Herslip looked beyond the riders standing by their horses to how the land lay in that direction, and then at the ridge indicated by Rood. A question started to form in Herslip's eyes, and then it came to him. "Up on that ridge they'll be looking into the sun. Some'll be there, but the main shooters will be east of the road. Wet or not, let's head in there." He swung into the saddle, his wet Levi's gripping at his legs and kind of gimping his toes in his wet boots. Then he headed out, to have Rood catch up to him.

"The lower side of that ridgeline, Rollie, slopes up gradually. I chased a cow up there once. As I recall there's some junipers and not much else, a few boulders too."

They covered the first two or so miles at a brisk canter, and from here everyone knew as the long ridge opened up to them that the attention of anyone up there would be focused on the road. Still, it didn't shake away their apprehension.

Soon Rood's jabbing hand revealed some horses

206

ground-hitched in an old dry wash, and he whispered, though he could have spoken louder, "Nobody's keepin' watch on them hosses." He eyed the rising ground of the sloping ridge to where it tapered off, gauging it to be around fifty rods in length with ample cover for them to keep saddle-bound.

"There!" exclaimed Otto Franc, going for his long-gun.

Someone had just stood up to steady his rifle against a juniper tree, and even as the rancher was levering a shell into the breech of his rifle, Sheriff Herslip's rifle was sounding, the slug screeching out of the barrel punching into the back of the man on the ridge. Barely had the crackling reverberations died away than a host of other rifles began punching holes in the quiet of morning.

"Lord a'mighty!" muttered Jimbo Rood as he brought his horse plunging up-slope.

When the offhand horse of a pair pulling the buggy began tossing its head and breaking stride, Deal Calloway knew trouble was brewing. Back along the road as they'd passed, birds had flitted up from tufts of brush and trees. But that hadn't happened where Deal was at the moment, just coming onto a high ridge dominating the immediate terrain, and he was about to call out to the pair of front riders when a rifle boomed, not all that far away. He started sawing on the reins in an attempt to bring his horses off the road to some sheltering rocks when more rifles opened up.

Quickly he wrenched out his sixgun and slammed it down on Soddy Kling's bonneted head. The man tumbled out of the buggy to lay still alongside the road. It was a cruel act, but it would keep the hardcase alive in the coming firefight. "Pile out!" he shouted to the others, as it seemed their buggy was the particular target of the ambushers.

One of them didn't make it to the rocks. Lem Waverly, a cowhand in for the meeting, went down hard, but still kept on crawling as Deal dropped down alongside to offer his body as a shield.

"Where'd they get you?"

"In the leg, dammit, Calloway. Been hurt so many times the last few years I'm beginnin' to like it." Another slug from a rifle gouged into the ground near his head throwing up debris and chippy little rocks.

Now, low as Deal and the others were on the ground, the ambushers east of the road were lifting to reveal themselves, but to Deal and those trying to survive they were nigh invisible, because of the bright sunlight coming at them. At last they were behind some large rocks, with Waverly grunting in pain when his wounded leg bumped against one of the rocks.

As Waverly busied himself with the task of tying his bandanna around the upper part of his leg, Deal was hammering bullets easterly. "Cowley . . . what happened to Cowley?" When he looked to the north he grimaced, for one of the horses was down, and he couldn't tell if it was Cowley's or the deputy's gelding.

Wait a minute, Deal exclaimed silently, *that first shot came from west of here.* He twisted on his back and stabbed his eyes at the ridge looming over them at a sharp angle, and as he did, he was staring up at Jock La Prele, who was getting set to fire his rifle again.

Only Deal managed to fire first. The second time he

triggered his sixgun it struck on an empty chamber, and he threw himself away from the rock just as La Prele opened up.

"Lem, your sixgun!"

Without hesitating the cowhand tossed it over to Deal, who began firing up at the gunfighter, rapidly, desperately, scoring hits on La Prele's body. One final slug from Deal's gun knocked the rifle away from the gunfighter's weakening grip, and he stumbled sideways, one boot clawing over rimrock. Then Jock La Prele was falling. It seemed just before he struck into the rocks below the dead eyes of the gunfighter bored into Deal's. There was a lull in the firing. Deal keened his ears questioningly to the distant and unexpected cry of a loon.

The silence held, briefly. Then more rifle fire came from east of the road, which soon died away. Cautiously Deal pushed to his feet. The bitter scent of cordite filled his nostrils, pushing away the murky smell of rocks and soil. He moved out onto the road to find Soddy Kling stirring into wakefulness.

"Calloway!"

A glance up at the ridge showed riders he knew strung along it, and he wondered how many had been hit. He detected movement further along the road. This turned out to be Elmo Cowley holding his left arm close to his body, the deputy trailing behind as they began to converge on Deal.

He said, "That was about as close as they come, Elmo."

"Too darned close. Took a slug just above the elbow. Anybody else get hit?"

"Waverly—don't know about those with Herslip."

"I have to say, Deal," said Cowley through his pain,

"that I owe you my thanks. If I woulda had my way, I'da kept them locked in jail back there. I owe her an apology too—Cleo Blaine."

Now riders had come down from the ridge, others in from the east, and these men were holding rifles on two hardcases they'd captured. When they got closer, Deal said loudly, "How about that Englishman, Clareton, did anybody see him?"

"Nope," muttered Herslip as he dismounted.

When Deal received the same response from the others, he knew that once again Thomas Clareton had eluded being killed or captured. And Deal said, "Cleo? This bastard's just crazy enough to take a gun to her, and the others. Jimbo, can I borrow your hoss as I'm makin' tracks back to Meeteetse."

"Calloway, maybe you should wait for us." But, to Sheriff Cowley's dismay, Deal had already wheeled the bronc around and was galloping away.

Eighteen

Once they cleared the shading porch of a two-story mercantile store, Deputy Sheriff Pat Delsing gestured toward the telegraph office set back from the street in the middle of a big lot making up an acre of level ground. Beyond this lay a string of business places on Main Street. With Delsing was the boy who'd delivered the telegram that said that more messages citing the misdeeds of Thomas Clareton and his hired killers were coming in over the line.

That first telegram had cleared the woman walking at Delsing's side and her brother of any crimes, and the deputy felt a sort of embarrassed respect for her. He didn't quite know how to apologize.

There were benches to either side of the front door, where the men Cleo Blaine had hired, Cholach and Wardell, decided to wait while the others trooped inside.

"Shorty," Delsing said, "this is Mrs. Blaine. Her brother, Dave Webster."

The telegraph operator barely glanced up. He was writing down what was coming over the line on a pad of yellow paper. He just said curtly, "Howdy," gesturing to some messages he'd written down, and Delsing reached over the counter to lift them off the desk.

Now all of them moved to a high writing desk up by the front window. Delsing spread the messages out for everyone's benefit. The messages had been relayed out of Cheyenne by the U.S. Marshal's office, and they cut right to the bone, requesting that Sheriff Elmo Cowley detain certain men.

"Man," uttered the deputy, "there are a lot of them. La Prele . . . the Claretons . . . Kling . . . Green—every one considered to be armed and dangerous."

"A lot of them are dead," ventured Dave Webster. "Some killed by their own kind."

As she read the messages, Cleo Blaine's thoughts were away from Meeteetse and on the men who'd left with Sheriff Elmo Cowley. Mostly, though, they centered on her concern for Deal Calloway. Could he be risking his life only because, as he'd told her out at Lonetree Ranch, an error of judgement on his part had led to the death of her U.S. marshal brother? It was only because of Deal that they had been taken from that jail and at least given a chance to tell their side to Sheriff Cowley. She laid her hand on Delsing's forearm and said, "Do you know if Jock La Prele has left town?"

"Yup, 'cause they've cleared out of that hotel near as I could learn long 'fore sunup."

"What about Thomas Clareton? Did he go along?"

"He ain't at his hotel either, Missus Blaine. But I did catch a glimpse earlier this mornin' of that woman, Jules, I reckon her name is, headin' over to Clareton's land office."

Nodding, she glanced at her brother, who was wearing his gun belt again, as were the men outside, and she

212

could see the matching worry in his eyes. Today Cleo had on a low-crowned western hat and a brown leather coat which concealed a Beals .31 caliber pocket revolver. Even before going in search of those who murdered her brother she'd been proficient with firearms. On the trail she would try her hand at blasting apart bottles, or fire the Beals at tin cans, with the hope that one day she'd line up her sights on either Jock La Prele or those Englishmen. The Beals didn't have the kicking power of a bigger caliber gun. But still, if a slug from it hit a man in a vital spot, it would take him out. Any lingering doubts about whether she could actually pull down on someone were swept away when her husband had been killed.

Down in Colorado Cleo had seen some old newspaper photographs of both Thomas and Francis Clareton. She let her eyes go to one of the messages scrawling out a description of the younger Clareton, Thomas. Just a mess of words, she mused, for he was older now, and had probably toned down both his appearance and high style of living. But she would know this vicious killer anywhere. How brazen of Clareton to push up here to Meeteetse, while the lying words of La Prele had almost caused her to be lynched.

Dave Webster gazed studiously at his sister, and he murmured, "You're thinking about him again."

"Yes," she said tautly, "about the one man who's caused so much misery. You can bet he didn't go along with La Prele this morning. He's here in town someplace. I know it."

"Could be, Mrs. Blaine," said Deputy Pat Delsing. "Trouble is, I'm the only lawman left in town. But what

I could do is make the rounds of the livery stables. Could be he rented a hoss and headed out."

"If you could do that," said Dave Webster. "We could catch up with you at the jail."

"I wouldn't wander around too much, folks. Everyone still believes you're outlaws."

"Thank you for your concern," smiled Cleo, her smile holding as the deputy headed away.

"So you think he's still holdin' in here . . ."

"I've ridden too many hard miles tracking after him, Dave. He's foxier now, probably fattened out with his belt holding in a beer keg of a belly, but I just know he hasn't left town."

"But he's planning to leave, Cleo. This Simone Jules—perhaps she can help us."

"Let's check her out." She piled the messages on top of one another and brought them over to hand them to the telegraph operator, who said curtly, "I'll see they're delivered to the sheriff's office. I couldn't help overhearing what you folks were jawin' about. In case you forgot, the stage pulls out around eleven this morning. Gent you're after could board at the last minute and be gone 'fore anybody knows it." Then another message coming over the telegraph line pulled him back to his desk.

And Cleo Blaine went out the front door ahead of her brother, where she turned around abruptly to say, "You can read me pretty good, brother of mine."

"That you were thinkin' the same thing as that telegraph operator, about going over to watch the stage leave town. Yup, reason I didn't mention it to that deputy sheriff. We can kill two birds with one stone, as its a block north of Clareton's land office."

"Sure," said Cleo Blaine. "You and Joe can stop at the land office while Hank and I hike on up to the stagecoach office."

"Watch yourself."

"He's never seen me before." She fell into step with her brother, and added, "And you know, it's about time we changed all of that."

"The sad thing is, Cleo, Clareton probably doesn't remember a U.S. marshal named Ray Webster."

"If he shows, I'll sure as hell jolt his memory."

Only an old-timer whittling a piece of pine into a whistle in front of a Main Street saloon took note of the woman seated on a bench across the wide dusty street. The woman had gotten up once to go into Sardella's grocery store and come out again biting into an apple. The building next to the grocery store housed the stagecoach office. The eyes of the old-timer flicked to more interesting things, as here people were milling about.

While in the grocery store, a clock on a shelf behind one of the counters had told Cleo Blaine it was only twenty minutes after ten. She'd managed to hide her apprehension behind a smile she gave a clerk. Now as she eased down on the bench again, the stagecoach swung into view and came her way at a walk. The driver brought it in close to a porch with a galvanized tin roof that cast back reflected light from the morning sun. Clerks began piling luggage and parcels that locals wanted mailed. The man riding shotgun moved into the rear storage compartment at a crabbing walk as he secured more luggage on the roof of the coach. Cleo's eyes sifted through the people clustered in little groups in search of the Englishman, knowing with a fatalistic certainty that he was going to board that coach.

She took in Hank Wardell watching from across the street. He brought up his hand to rub a finger along the side of his long nose; his eyes also registered the fact that he hadn't spotted Thomas Clareton. Biting into the apple again, Cleo felt a stir of anxiety, or perhaps it was just a tinge of fear, that perhaps she wasn't capable of killing another human being, even though she'd downed deer and elk and on one memorable occasion a mountain lion.

Rising, she turned to peer into the store. The clock revealed it was ten before the hour. Those about to embark on the stagecoach were climbing aboard and settling in. There was an older woman of remarkable bulk, and with a large bosom, clothed from head to shod feet all in black; a rancher with a sparse, bony face; two men in vested suits. The shotgun came out with a strongbox, which he lifted over his head to have the driver grasp and shove it in under his long seat. Most of the crowd was still present, enjoying the ritual of stagecoach-watching, a break in tedious lives.

Then Cleo Blaine stiffened. She had risen and had moved to the edge of the shaded porch to get a closer look at who was getting on board the coach. Now a cold chill gripped her as it had that time when she'd been waiting for that puma to show. Then, without warning, from the far side of the stage office there appeared Thomas Clareton, gripping a couple of valises. He strode quickly to where a clerk was holding the stagecoach door open and sort of facing the Englishman.

The clerk said, "Oh, I see you've purchased a ticket,

216

sir?" Now he called up to the shotgun, "Will, here's some more luggage."

Across the street, Hank Wardell's view of the front of the office was blocked by the stagecoach, and he had no idea that Clareton had arrived and was about to clamber into the coach. His eyes were riveted to Cleo Blaine, who was starting to move along the boardwalk, and when she called out, concern for the woman brought Wardell into the street even as his eyes chanced to pick up on Cleo's brother and Joe Cholach coming in from the south.

"Damn you, you murdering bastard!" Cleo shouted again. "Yes, you Mr. Clareton!"

Thomas Clareton had never seen Cleo Blaine before, but he'd been drinking the morning away while lurking at an edge of town saloon. Now he said sneeringly, "Lady, I resent your tone of voice. I'm known here as a respectable businessman. And I'm about to board this stage."

"No, Clareton, you're not leaving!"

The shotgun, staring from Clareton to the woman, threw down, "Mister, we've got to pull out."

Suddenly Clareton became aware of the two men pushing through those crowding along the street. A sixth sense told him they were part of this and that he must end it quickly. But he wasn't thinking clearly; he hadn't been, it seemed, ever since he'd murdered his brother. Recklessly now he jerked a hand inside his black frock coat for the holstered .36 model Navy Colt. It caught on his vest, but he managed to draw it out, only to find himself gaping at the sixgun held by the woman. Kill her, a voice screamed in his frenzied mind.

"You meddling . . ." He couldn't believe what was

217

happening. The gun in her hand was bucking, and suddenly there was crimson spattering the front of his starched white shirt. He tried reaching for the stagecoach door, but somehow it eluded his groping hand. His anger at what was happening bared his teeth. He was struck again, dead center, where the lower point of his ribcage touched upon his stomach. Somehow he seemed incapable of firing back, as something seemed wrong with his right hand and with his legs.

Cleo Blaine screamed out, though she seemed unaware of it, "You killed my brother, U.S. Marshal Ray Webster, damn you! Used hot tar to kill him!"

In his dying moments that particular night down in Colorado came to Thomas Clareton. And for just a moment he was there, holding a lighted torch, laughing at his intended prey. He tried laughing now, a confused jargon of sound, and then it struck him that now it was his turn to die. As Thomas Clareton was falling, horror gaped his eyes wide open, for it seemed he'd just been given a glimpse of the hot fires that were Hell.

Staring down at him, Cleo Blaine let her gunhand drop to her side. In around her came her brother and Cholach, then Hank Wardell. The only sound was made by the frightened horses trying to break away. The coach rolled ahead a few feet, and when it did, Cleo found herself taking in an incoming rider. At first she wasn't sure, then she saw that it was Deal Calloway moving into the space just vacated by the coach. From the misery etched on Cleo's face he knew what had taken place.

Deal looked around at the silent faces, and he said simply and plainly, while nodding down at the body, "That man's wanted for killin' a U.S. marshal."

Nineteen

Deal Calloway didn't see Cleo Blaine the rest of the week, as he was giving his testimony to a federal judge and the sheriffs of Big Horn and Park Counties. The hearing was held in the town hall. The only other person allowed in there was a recorder the judge had brought along. Then it was over, and Deal took his leave.

One thing in Deal's favor was that none of the telegraphs fired up from Colorado mentioned him as being involved down there. Perhaps, Elmo Cowley had mused to Deal, his luck was changing for the better. They were at a saloon unwinding from all that had happened, and Cowley said, "That judge kind of favors what you've done."

"At least my running days are over. But as far as settling here in the basin—just don't know, Elmo."

"Things'll die down. The Holters pulled in late yesterday afternoon. By rights I should go over and see them."

"Lon looks right fit again. Probably fit enough to go back to ranching."

"I expect he'll do that, Elmo."

"I thought you wanted to buy Lonetree."

"Once all that I said in that hearing gets out, Marge and Lon will want to wash their hands of this 'poke. They knew some of what I did, but not all the details. They'll want to see me move on. Which is just as well, I reckon."

"You feeling sorry for yourself again."

"Just the unvarnished truth, Sheriff Cowley. Living with half-lies and the such isn't much of an existence. At least, if and when I can leave, I can face the truth about myself. One thing too, this scar I'm stuck with, don't pay much of a mind to it anymore."

Sheriff Cowley laid an idle glance on the stirring batwings, and then a smile etched across his face when Marge Holter entered the saloon, followed by her husband. He rose, as did Deal, and Cowley swept the hat from his head and said, "Marge, welcome home. Place has sure seemed mighty lonesome without you and Lon around." He gave Marge Holter a hug, then shook Lon's hand.

"Elmo," she said, "could we have a word with Deal?"

"Why, I was just about to head back to my office."

As the sheriff left, Deal found himself exchanging pleasantries with the Holters, all of them settling around the table, a few others in the saloon going back to what they were doing before the Holters arrived. "I," said Deal, "well, a lot has happened since I left Old Thermopolis."

"From what we've heard, it's over," said Lon, as he caught the bartender's eye, and he ordered coffee. "Deal, what you did only justified our trust in you."

"Yes," said Marge Holter, "you're a top hand, and a dear friend. She thinks so too."

Puzzlement flared in Deal's eyes.

"Tell me, Mr. Calloway, do you still have plans to buy Lonetree—"

"After all that's happened I don't expect I have much of a credit rating in the basin, an' not only amongst bankers either."

She said tartly, "That isn't what I asked. Well, what about it, we want to sell out to you."

"Mrs. Holter, Lon, I . . . well I reckon I still entertain some thoughts along that line. But Lonetree, she's worth a lot of money I don't quite have. By the way, you mentioned a she, whoever that is?"

As the bartender brought over a tray holding two cups and a pot of coffee, Marge Holter said, "I'd like some brandy in mine if you please; some top shelf stuff." Now she opened her purse and dipped a hand inside to lift out a large brown envelope. She extracted from the envelope two smaller envelopes, one of which she passed to her husband. "You may have the honors, Lon."

"Reckon so," he grinned through the mischievous glint in his eyes. From the envelopes he extracted a thick sheaf of papers and unfolded them. He explained, "The deed to Lonetree. Somebody just paid cash money for it." He pointed out to Deal the name of the new owner.

"That's my name?" He looked up in disbelief at the pair of them, groping for some explanation to all of this.

The answer he received was to have Marge Holter hand him the second envelope. Then she drank a little coffee, and setting her cup down, said, "Come on, Lon, we've got some errands to run. And, Mr. Calloway, we expect the new owner of Lonetree to spring for dinner over at the Rawhider Hotel."

Alone at the table, Deal took another hard, disbelieving look at the piece of paper giving him ownership of Lonetree Ranch. Now he opened the other envelope, to find that it contained a letter addressed to him. Before reading it, he turned to the last page and saw that it was from Cleo Blaine.

"My Dear Mr. Calloway," he began reading silently.

Down near the bottom of the first page he learned she had purchased Lonetree only to deed it over to him, as she explained, her attempt to thank him for all he had done at the risk of his own life. That someday, the letter went on, she would come back to the Big Horn Basin. But that for now she must return to Oklahoma and sort out her affairs and thoughts for the future.

The last page held the most startling news of all for Deal Calloway: that Cleo felt she'd fallen in love with him. At last when he had finished reading the letter, Deal laid it before him on the table, a man still benumbed by what had just happened to him.

He did take the Holters out to dinner.

And when he went in search of Cleo Blaine, he found to his dismay that she had left Meeteetse for Oklahoma.

"A lady, same as Marge Holter," he remarked the next day, when he was on his way out to claim ownership of Lonetree—and on his way to begin a new life.

FOLLOW THE SEVENTH CARRIER

TRIAL OF THE SEVENTH CARRIER (3213, $3.95)
The enemies of freedom are on the verge of dominating the world with oil blackmail and the threat of poison gas attack. *Yonaga*'s officers lay desperate plans to strike back. Leading a ragtag fleet of revamped destroyers and a single antique WWII submarine, the great carrier must charge into a sea of blood and death in what becomes the greatest trial of the Seventh Carrier.

REVENGE OF THE SEVENTH CARRIER (3631, $3.99)
With the help of an American carrier, *Yonaga* sails vast distances to launch a desperate surprise attack on the enemy's poison gas works. But a spy is at work. The enemy seems to know too much and a bloody battle is fought. Filled with murderous rage, *Yonaga*'s officers exact a terrible revenge.

ORDEAL OF THE SEVENTH CARRIER (3932, $3.99)
Even as the Libyan madman calls for peaceful negotiations, an Arab battle group steams toward the shores of Japan. With good men from all over the world flocking to her colors, *Yonaga* prepares to give battle. The two forces clash off the island of Iwo Jima where it is carrier against carrier in a duel to the death — and *Yonaga,* sustaining severe damage, endures its bloodiest ordeal in the fight for freedom's cause.

*

Other Zebra Books by Peter Albano

THE YOUNG DRAGONS (3904, $4.99)
It is June 25, 1944. American forces attack the island of Saipan. Two young fighting men on opposite sides, Michael Carpelli and Takeo Nakamura, meet in the flaming hell of battle that will inevitably bring them face-to-face in a final fight to the death. Here is the epic battle that decided the war against Japan as told by a man who was there.